IT'S A GIRL THING

HOW TO STAY HEALTHY, SAFE, AND IN CHARGE

IT'S A GIRL THING

HOW TO STAY HEALTHY, SAFE, AND IN CHARGE

by MAVIS JUKES

illustrations by
Debbie Tilley

Alfred A. Knopf   New York

THIS IS A BORZOI BOOK PUBLISHED BY ALFRED A. KNOPF, INC.
Text copyright © 1996 by Mavis Jukes
Illustrations copyright © 1996 by Debbie Tilley
Cover art copyright © 1996 by Kyrsten Brooker

http://www.randomhouse.com/

Library of Congress Cataloging-in-Publication Data
Jukes, Mavis.
It's a girl thing : how to stay healthy, safe, and in charge / by Mavis Jukes ;
illustrations by Debbie Tilley.
p. cm.
ISBN 0-679-87392-9 (trade pbk.)
ISBN 0-679-94325-0 (lib. bdg.)
ISBN 0-679-88771-7 (pbk.)
1. Teenage girls—United States—Juvenile literature. 2. Puberty—United
States—Juvenile literature. 3. Sex instruction for girls—United States.
[1. Puberty. 2. Sex instruction for girls.]
I. Tilley, Debbie, ill. II. Title.
HQ798.J85   1996
305.23'5—dc20   93-40296
Printed in the United States of America
10 9 8 7 6 5 4 3

*To Marguerite Jukes—for hosting all the Ladies'
Business Club meetings of my childhood, whether
she wanted to or not. I love you, Mom!*

XOXOXOXO

Contents

Acknowledgments

Thanks to everyone who helped with this book; thanks for the stories bravely contributed.

Special thanks to:

Sonia Bledsoe, M.D.—for ideas, medical review, and friendship throughout the writing process.

Deirdre Joy Pearl, M.D.—for medical review in the area of pediatric medicine.

Lisa Bernard, M.D.—for medical review in the area of obstetrics and gynecology.

Natalie Rubinton, Ph.D.—for review in the area of adolescent psychology.

Amy Bowles, doctoral candidate in American Studies at George Washington University and specialist in Feminist Young Adult Literature—for compiling the list for further reading.

Jill Davis—for insight and advice.

Introduction

In 1958, I was eleven years old. I was in the fifth grade. I wore a little bit of pink lipstick, but not to school. My school clothes were dresses with bows in the back, and ankle socks with buckle shoes—pants weren't allowed. At home, I wore blue jeans with the cuffs rolled up, or shorts and a cotton shirt, and I went barefoot. I wore plastic barrettes in my hair. They came on paper cards: two yellow, two pink, two blue.

Even though I was eleven, I still played cowboys. I pretended my bicycle was a horse. I played hide-and-seek with my brother and sister. After supper, I sat on the porch and watched the fireflies blink.

I was private about my body and didn't let anybody see me naked. I had two small breasts. I had a few pubic hairs—not many. In the mornings, I'd put on some of my mother's deodorant.

I knew all the basics about womanhood, because my mother never locked me out of her bathroom. I was a member of an exclusive organization: the Ladies' Business Club.

Most mornings my mother took a shower, but sometimes she just gave herself a quick sponge bath. Naked, she filled the sink and washed her armpits, crotch, and rear with a soapy washcloth. She rinsed herself, carefully wringing out the washcloth, often humming a tune.

A few days each month, after she had bathed and dried off, my mother climbed into a thin elastic belt. She turned it around so there was one hook in the front and one in the back. Then she hooked a big white pad onto the clips.

Next, she put on a garter belt. Then she put on cotton underwear and pulled the garters, which were attached to elastic ribbons, down through the leg holes. She attached stockings, which had seams up the back, to the garters. She bent over when she fastened her bra so her breasts were in the right place when she stood up.

She then pulled a slip over her head and put on a blouse and buttoned it. She stepped into a skirt and zipped it up the side. She put on high-heeled shoes. Then she brushed her hair. Finally, she put on perfume and lipstick, earrings, and beads or a pin.

Later, if I happened to walk into the bathroom when it was time for my mom to change her pad, she wouldn't seem embarrassed. She would just sit on the pot, chatting about this or that.

I would watch with interest as she unhooked the pad from the elastic belt, front and back, rolled it up, wrapped it in newspaper, and threw it into the trash. Then I would hand her a new pad out of the box in the bathroom cupboard. She would attach it to the hooks on the elastic belt. Sometimes she would sprinkle on a little deodorant powder, which came in a small tin can.

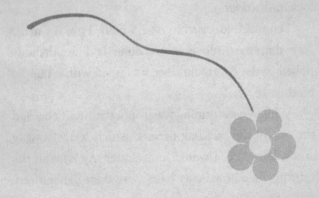

The Rules

The Ladies' Business Club was, as its name suggests, strictly for girls. My chapter had only two members: my mom and me.

Meetings were held on the spur of the moment in my mother's bathroom or in her bedroom, but never when my parents were together—only when my mom was there alone.

The club rules were these: I could come into the bathroom when my mom was bathing or going to the bathroom—but she couldn't when I was.

My mother always respected the rules. Besides, I locked the door.

Before I undressed to take a bath, I always made sure that the little hole someone had accidentally poked in the bathroom door was filled with a blob of toothpaste.

While I was running water into the tub, I checked the size of my budding breasts, which were growing at a snail's pace. I would look under my arms in the mirror to see how many hairs were there. There were just a few.

In the bath, I would borrow big handfuls of shampoo bubbles from my head and make two piles on my chest. This would help me to see how I would look one day when my breasts would be, well, huge.

I would soap up my body and write my initials in cursive letters on my skin. Then I'd draw, maybe a heart or a flower. When I dried myself, I would fluff up my pubic hair with the towel to make it look fuller than it actually was.

About this book

Not every girl is as happy about growing breasts, pubic hair, and underarm hair as I was. Some girls are embarrassed and wish their bodies weren't changing.

Some girls talk openly with their families and close friends about the changes that come with growing up, and others don't.

Knowing what's going on with your body is reassuring; it also can help keep you healthy and safe as you grow into a woman.

This book talks about breasts, pubic hair, underarm hair, underarm perspiration, and menstruation.

It talks about bras, deodorant, tampons, pads, and other things some girls and women think about, like makeup and high-heeled shoes.

You will learn about sex, sexuality, pregnancy, and birth control. You will learn about sexually transmitted diseases, including AIDS.

Do you feel ready to explore these topics in a book? If you're not sure, ask your parents whether they would recommend *It's a Girl Thing* for you. If they do, remember to ask questions and talk to a parent, a doctor, a teacher, a school counselor, or another trusted adult about anything in this book that you would like clarified or explained.

Chapter 1

Breasts and Bras

❁ POPPING THE QUESTION

When I was eleven I wanted a bra, but I was too shy to ask my mother for one. I would practice the question over and over again to myself.

I would stand beside my mother and dry all the dishes, thinking I might at any moment turn to her and casually say, "Mom? Can I have a bra?"

But the words didn't come.

Finally, one day my mother and her friend Agnes were sitting on the porch in the wicker chairs with flowered cushions, drinking iced tea. I stood in the doorway, kicking open the screen door and stopping it from banging shut again with the toe of my shoe.

1

"Do you want something, sweetie?" my mother asked.

"Yes," I told her through the screen. "I want a bra." I hurried back into the house and sat on the edge of my bed and blushed. Had I actually asked for it? In front of Agnes?

The next day, my mother and I went to a small clothing store on Main Street. With the help of a saleswoman, we selected the only bra that was available in size 28AA.

I went into the dressing room alone and pulled the curtain closed tightly, so nobody could peek.

I took the bra out of its small box, which had a picture of a girl wearing the bra on the front. It was white—maybe the whitest thing I'd ever seen in my life besides snow. There was a tiny pink flower in the middle, with a fake pearl in the center. The bra smelled new—and delicious!

I leaned over to put it on the way my mother did—although this wasn't necessary, since I was practically flat. With difficulty, I hooked the little metal loop into the clasp at the back. I looked in the mirror and adjusted the straps so the cups of the bra wouldn't look so empty. I turned to the side, then to the front again. I put on my shirt and carried the empty box out of the dressing room.

I had a bra—and I loved it. And I loved the idea of wearing it so much that I slept in it for the first couple of weeks, taking it off only to wash it.

❀ BREAST BUDS

At some point after about age eight, a girl will notice bumps behind her nipples. They indicate that her breasts are beginning to form.

The appearance of these bumps, called *breast buds*, is often one of the first signs that a girl is beginning to go through *puberty*.

Pubic Hair

A friend of mine told me that she was in the shower, lathering up, when she noticed her little girl peering at her from around the edge of the shower curtain.

"Mom?" asked the little girl. "When I grow up, will I have feathers, too?"

Pubic hair begins to grow at about the time that breast buds form. It begins as a fuzzy patch that thickens and spreads out—eventually carpeting a small area between our legs in the shape of an upside-down triangle. Pubic hair can be curly or straight; it can be black, brown, red, or blond. It doesn't really have a purpose—other than decoration!

WHAT IS PUBERTY?

Puberty is the name for a set of changes that occur between the ages of about eight to about sixteen. *Hormones* (chemicals produced by our bodies) cause these changes, which are both physical and emotional. Going through puberty is the start of becoming sexually mature. Girls develop breasts, grow taller, begin *menstruation* ("having your period"), and develop additional body hair.

Going through puberty means that the parts of your body that will enable you to have a baby are beginning to function.

Boys also go through puberty. For more information about puberty for boys, see page 78.

✿ We're One of a Kind

Breasts come in a variety of shades and shapes and sizes: large, medium, small, very small, dark, pale, full, flat.

Nipples come in many shades and shapes and sizes, too. Some nipples are brown, some are plum colored, some are dark pink, some are pale pink. Some nipples cover a large area of the breast; others cover very little.

Our breasts are unique to our bodies because we're one of a kind. There's no particular way breasts are "supposed" to look. Breasts are beautiful—big or small, dark or light, round or flat. Besides being beautiful, they have functions that relate to sex and human reproduction.

When touched, breasts can produce pleasant sexual feelings.

They also can produce milk after a woman has a baby. The baby drinks the milk by sucking on the mom's nipple. This is called *nursing,* or *breast-feeding.* When a baby nurses, the mother feels a gentle tugging sensation. Normally it doesn't hurt, unless the baby has teeth and decides to take a nibble!

Sometimes, though, women experience soreness of their nipples when they first begin to nurse.

Some women have a few hairs that grow out of the small glands at the edge of the *areola,* the dark area around the nipple. These hairs are normal. Small, pimplelike glands can also be found around the nipple. These are also normal. Hairs and these glands should be left alone.

Sometimes a girl develops a breast bud on one

side first. If this happens to you, don't worry, the other side will catch up. Breasts take a few years to develop fully, and they don't have to begin growing at the same time to end up being about equal in size.

Many younger girls feel that breasts will be a lovely addition to their bodies, but some girls are embarrassed about growing breasts—at first. Lots of girls worry about their breasts being too big or too small, or that they are starting to grow too early or too late.

There's no way of knowing what size your breasts will eventually be. But whatever their size when fully developed, they will be right for you.

Breast Surgery

Medical procedures are available to modify breast size and shape. Some women, including women who are made physically uncomfortable because of having extremely large breasts, explore this alternative with their doctors.

❧ Bras

The main work of a bra is to support the breasts. Many girls and women feel more comfortable when their breasts are held snugly against their chests, especially when they walk, run, jump, work, or play sports.

A bra also provides privacy against peeking when a girl has on a sleeveless shirt, and it helps to keep nipples from showing through a thin shirt.

These reasons—plus just plain wanting one for the fun of it, or because other girls have one—are all legitimate answers to the question of why you might want a bra.

Not every girl wants to wear a bra. Some girls prefer to "go braless," or to wear a tank top or T-shirt instead of a bra under their clothes.

❧ Fitting a Bra

Bra sizes are indicated with a number plus a letter.

The numbers (28, 30, 32, 34, 36, 38, 40, 42, 44, and so on) represent how big your chest is in inches as measured under your breasts, across your ribs. The basic rule is this: If you measure an even number, such as 28, then add four inches to find your number size. You will probably find that a size 32 bra will fit. If you measure an odd number, such as 27, then add five inches to find your number size—you will probably find that a size 32 bra will also fit.

How do you get this measurement? With a tape measure. If you don't have a tape measure at home, you can measure yourself with a string and then measure the string with a yardstick or a ruler.

Specially marked measuring tapes are available in most stores that sell bras. And in many stores, the saleswomen have been trained to measure for bra sizes. This is done over your shirt to protect your privacy. If you don't want to be measured, say so. Ask for the tape so you can measure yourself.

The letters correspond to the size of the breasts and are called cup sizes. AAA and AA cup sizes are the smallest sizes and are usually worn by girls who want a bra but don't need one yet for support.

Sizes A, B, C, D, and DD/E are the other letter sizes that are generally available.

To find your letter size, measure your chest with the tape measure passing across your nipples. If the measurement is the same as your number size, your cup size will probably be AAA or AA. If it's one inch bigger, the cup will be an A; two inches bigger, a B; three inches bigger, a C; four inches bigger, a D; five inches bigger, DD or DD/E.

❀ Choosing a Bra

In the 28 to 30, AAA and AA, size range, there may be only one or two choices of styles and fabrics. In sizes 32 and up, there is usually a large selection, including colors and prints.

Number and letter sizing is just a guide, not a guarantee that the bra will fit. Always try on a bra before you buy it. The fit depends on the fabric and the style. Every bra company has a slightly different idea of what, for example, a size 34B is. So be prepared to spend some time in the dressing room.

Choose a bra that's comfortable—not too tight around your body or too small in the cup. A bra that's too tight will drive you crazy!

Find the cup size that you feel happy with. How does it look with your shirt on? If the cup size is too big, the cup will collapse and look wrinkled, and you might not be happy with the look.

Some bras are made of soft, stretchy material and

allow for growing; many girls choose these for first bras. "Sports bras" are usually stretchy elastic, which offers support for active exercise. They should not be so tight that they cause a lot of pressure on your breasts.

Some bras have wires under the cups; these are called underwire bras. Bras with underwires tend to be more expensive and may be uncomfortable, especially if they don't fit well.

Do you want a bra with a clasp in the front or the back? Both options are available in most sizes.

Washing a Bra

Many bras, especially fancy ones, are delicate and should be washed by hand instead of in the washing machine. Check the label for washing instructions.

To wash a bra by hand, fill a sink with warm water. You can use a little liquid dish soap, some mild detergent, or just the soap in the soap dish. Wash, rinse well, and hang the bra up to dry. Most bras will dry overnight.

❧"Falsies"

As I entered my teens, I felt cheated by Mother Nature in the breast department. One day, a neighbor stopped by the house with a stack of hand-me-down clothes. She held up a two-piece bathing suit.

"Think you would ever wear something like this?" she asked.

No, I wouldn't wear anything like it; it was the wrong size, out of style, and a weird shade of blue. To be polite, I looked it over anyway, and discovered that inside the top were foam rubber inserts—which used to be known as "falsies"—to enhance the bustline.

"Yes, I think I might wear this," I told her. "Or parts of it," I added to myself.

As soon as the woman left, I disappeared into my room with the bathing suit and a small pair of scissors.

In a flash, I cut the foam rubber inserts out of the top of the bathing suit and put them into my own bra. And I transferred them from bra to bathing suit to bra, secretly enhancing my bustline, most of the way through high school.

It was a pain trying to hide my falsies from the other girls when we dressed for gym. I had to develop a routine to change from my school clothes to my gym suit—which was a jumpsuit with short pants. I would undress down to my slip, then step into my uniform and button it up. Somehow, I would then sn-e-e-e-ak off my slip. I think I had to pull it through the sleeve.

Don't ask me how I managed to put it back on.

After a while, I became almost a prisoner of my falsies; once I started wearing them, I couldn't stop. I refused to undress around anybody, including my best friend, who cheerily stuffed socks in her bra without the slightest embarrassment.

In the summer, I spent a lot of time sitting by the edge of the pool, dangling my legs in the water before slipping quietly in. I wouldn't have dreamed of jumping or diving in, fearful that my falsies would spring out of my bathing suit top and float to the surface, like little life preservers.

❀ Sallie's Falsies Disaster

When my friend Sallie was a kid, she went to summer camp. One year, she secretly helped herself to her mother's foam rubber falsies and stashed them in her suitcase.

At camp, she tucked the falsies into her bathing

suit and walked to the pond where kids were swimming, supervised by the lifeguard—a cute teenage boy. She strolled up and tested the water with her foot.

She then took a running leap off the dock into the water.

She kicked her way back up to the surface and blinked the water out of her eyes. Then she noticed that her mother's two bright white foam rubber falsies had popped out of her suit and set sail across the lake.

She took a deep breath and ducked back under the water, reappearing some distance away among the lily pads at the edge of the lake.

To her horror, she saw the lifeguard—this adorable guy wearing nothing but a small red swimsuit and a whistle around his neck—skimming her mother's falsies from the lake with a long aluminum pole with a net on the end.

"Well, now," he called out. "Who would these belong to?" The other kids swam closer to look; some began hooting and hollering.

"Whose on earth are these?" the lifeguard kept calling out.

Sallie silently lurked among the lily pads, watching and saying nothing.

✿ Padded Bras

Thirty years have passed since I slipped downstairs in the middle of the night and stuffed my foam rubber inserts way, *way* down into the bottom of the trash. The racks of padded bras in department stores sometimes seem tempting; occasionally, I stop and give a padded bra a squeeze—just for old times' sake.

It's sad but true that some girls and women still feel that breasts can be "too small."

Maybe your generation will be the one that "just says no" to padded bras. And falsies!

Chapter 2

Introducing ... YOUR Period!

❀ The Magic Moment

When I was a kid, we didn't have a dozen or more different kinds of beltless pads to choose from. There were two brands of pads, both worn with elastic belts.

The pads came in pale, pastel-colored boxes, designed not to call undue attention to themselves on the drugstore shelf. The advertising of pads—called sanitary napkins—was subtle. One ad simply showed a picture of the box and said:

"...because..."

Because why?

Nobody knew.

In the small town where I grew up, pads could be bought only at the drugstore, and they were kept behind the counter out of view. The pharmacist, *always* a man, would discreetly discuss the weather or some other topic while taking money, giving change, and hiding the large box of pads in a brown paper bag.

I knew that someday I would go into the drugstore by myself to buy pads, and I knew that I would *not* say "pads," the way my mother did. I hated the word and wished she would refer to them simply by their brand name or by the words "sanitary napkins."

I would rehearse the procedure in my mind—how I might first look at the lipstick or nail polish and pick one. I would get money out of my change purse and walk over to the cash register and, just as the druggist was ringing up the sale, I'd say, as if I had forgotten, "Oh, and a box of sanitary napkins, please."

Yes, someday I would go to the drugstore by myself, but I began to wonder when this would be…

I waited hopefully to begin my period through the fifth, sixth, and seventh grades. By the time I got to the end of the seventh grade, it still hadn't started—and this began to interfere with the image I had of myself as a leader.

When my friend Ellen—whom I considered to be my physical equal—had her first period, I decided that the best way for me to handle the situation was to lie. So I told everybody who asked—and a few who didn't—that yes, of course, definitely, I had begun.

A few girls confided in me that they hadn't started their periods yet. And I confidently advised them not to worry, that sooner or later they would. And, sooner or later, they did—every last one of them.

Except me.

By the end of eighth grade, I didn't know a single other girl who hadn't started her period. At that point in my life, I had already been taught by my older brother how to drive a Packard and fly a Piper Cub plane.

But I was the only one of my friends who did not yet operate the machine in the girls' bathroom. There, for ten cents, they bought sanitary napkins…

…because…

They had started their periods.

And I hadn't!

One day in April, I sat at a table in the cafeteria having lunch with my friends. They were laughing and talking; I was feeling a little crummy. I got up to go to the bathroom.

I saw a little brownish red mark in my underwear. I looked at it closely. There it was—the actual dribble of blood I had been yearning and wishing for.

My heart pounding, I jumped up and hurried out of the booth. I found a dime in my skirt pocket. I put it in the machine and turned the handle. A beautiful little cardboard box dropped out.

I can't ever remember being so happy to open up a package. I pulled out a big, fat white pad with a blue line down the back and two long tails, and two tiny gold safety pins to attach the tails to the inside of my underwear.

I pinned it on and waddled out of the bathroom.

✿ MENSTRUATION

If you haven't accidentally barged into the bathroom when your mother or stepmother or aunt or grandmother or big sister happened to be changing a pad or putting in a tampon, or if you haven't talked with anyone about *menstruation*, there's something you need to know right away: Menstruation is normal. It usually begins when a girl is between the ages of nine and sixteen—most commonly at about age thirteen.

When a girl begins to menstruate, it means that her reproductive system has begun to work.

It takes a while, perhaps a year or two, for the

reproductive system to get into rhythm, but when it does, a girl menstruates about once a month.

When we say once a month, we mean about once every twenty-one to forty days. The range of days in a menstrual cycle varies, and not every girl or woman menstruates in a regular pattern, although most do. Many teens have irregular cycles.

All women eventually stop menstruating. Stopping altogether is called *menopause*. The changes that gradually lead to menopause begin some time after the age of forty. Menopause usually happens slowly, over the course of many months or years. The average age for stopping menstruation is fifty-one.

Starting to menstruate is a sign of good health, but my friend Milly didn't know that. She started her period before her mom had a chance to explain it to her. When she discovered blood in her underwear, she went into her bedroom, sat down, and wrote out a will.

Milly was in no danger. There was no cause for panic, and no reason to give away her comics collection.

Although menstruating involves bleeding, it's not like bleeding from a cut. There's just a small, set amount of bloody fluid that is released from the uterus through the *vagina*. It dribbles out slowly, first at the rate of a few teaspoons a day, and then less and less.

The Vagina

Sometimes a girl doesn't understand where her vagina is. This is no surprise. It's difficult to get into a position where you can see it.

If you haven't found your vagina yet, you can privately scout it out next time you're getting ready for a bath or shower. You can find it by sitting down with your legs apart. It helps to use a mirror.

Your vagina is just below the place where urine (pee) comes out of your body. In young girls, the opening of the vagina is usually, but not always, covered or partly covered by a fold of membrane called a *hymen*. Your vagina is like a soft, warm, moist passageway.

It is through the vagina that menstrual blood comes out. Girls and women catch this blood before it gets on their clothes or bedding by putting a pad into their underwear, or by using tampons, which are described on page 43. Some women use clean rags for pads.

The vagina is also the private place that is involved in having sex and becoming pregnant.

And, believe it or not, it's also the opening through which a baby is born.

☺UCH!

How can a baby fit through an opening that small? Believe me, this is a question that every pregnant woman asks herself—usually a number of times—throughout her pregnancy.

The walls of the vagina are very stretchy, and during pregnancy a woman's body goes through many subtle changes that make it easier for the baby to come out.

Still, anybody can easily put two and two together to figure out that getting a baby through an opening that small is a very tight squeeze.

❊The Uterus

Menstrual fluid leaves the body by way of the vagina, but it originally comes from the *uterus*. Your uterus is located inside your body, between your belly button (also called your navel) and your crotch. It's a small, expandable pear-shaped organ that is also sometimes called a *womb*. In girls, it's about as big as a walnut.

When a woman becomes pregnant, the uterus is where the baby grows—not in her stomach, which is the organ that both women and men have for digesting food.

Once a girl goes through puberty, her uterus makes a special lining of bloody tissue every month to prepare for a possible pregnancy.

If a pregnancy were to occur, the lining would nourish the embryo as it grew and developed inside the uterus. An *embryo* is a group of cells that grows into a *fetus,* which is the beginnings of a baby.

Pregnancy can occur only after male reproductive cells—called *sperm*—are introduced into the body of a female through her vagina. In other words, a woman can't become pregnant all on her own. Exactly how a woman becomes pregnant is discussed later in this book (see page 101).

If a woman or girl isn't pregnant, the lining of her uterus isn't needed to nourish an embryo, and the lining is released. Over about five days, it trickles out of the vagina as menstrual fluid.

And then the uterus begins to make a new lining all over again. Releasing the blood and tissue that lines the uterus each month is what menstruation is all about.

Female Sex Organs

Inner Sex Organs:
Two ovaries, two Fallopian (uterine) tubes, a uterus, a cervix (the bottom of the uterus), and a vagina make up the inner sex organs.

Outer Sex Organs:
The vulva includes the mons pubis, labia majora and minora, clitoris, vestibule of the vagina, and vestibular glands, described below.

The *mons pubis* is the rounded place where your pubic hair mainly grows, directly above your entire vaginal region. The *labia majora* are the two plump skin folds that come together and form the "lips" of the *vulva*; the *labia minora* are the two smaller folds of skin that surround the openings of the vagina and the urethra (where urine comes out of the body). The area around these openings defined by the two smaller folds of skin (labia minora) is the *vestibule*, and that's where the *vestibular glands* empty out (which can make the area slippery).

The *hymen* is a fold of mucous membrane that partially covers the entrance to the vagina.

The *clitoris*, a small "bump" located at the top of the vulva, is made up of erectile tissue. Erectile tissue is tissue that can temporarily become fuller and "harder." The clitoris, when stimulated, can cause feelings of intense physical, sexual pleasure, which may lead to an *orgasm* (discussed on page 91).

What Causes Menstruation to Begin

Each girl approaches puberty according to her own unique timetable, but the same basic things happen to every girl. The body increases its production of chemicals called *hormones*. These hormones start up and regulate the reproductive system, the body's system for producing children.

It may be helpful to think of the hormones as a signaling system, with hormones being the chemical messengers sent to tell certain parts of the body what to do. Hormones control growth, sex drive, and the body's reaction to stress. Both males and females produce hormones.

Nobody knows exactly what triggers puberty. But we do know that one of the first things that happens is that a gland called the *pituitary gland* sends out hormones that travel to the *ovaries*.

Ovaries are small, oval reproductive organs located inside a female's body, close to her uterus. Girls are born with two ovaries, which contain hundreds of thousands of tiny unripe *eggs*, each in a small sac.

When a girl's body is maturing sexually, a hormone called *follicle stimulating hormone* (FSH) from the pituitary gland acts as a signal to some of the eggs in the ovaries. These eggs then begin to mature and make their own hormone, called *estrogen*.

Over a period of many months, estrogen produced in the eggs travels through the bloodstream, activating changes in different parts of the girl's body. Along with hormones from the *adrenal glands*, estrogen gives signals for breasts to begin to form and be padded with protective fatty tissue and for pubic hair and underarm hair to grow. Estrogen also causes other, more subtle changes that are neither felt nor seen, like making the uterus grow.

Near the time when a girl is ready to have her first period, the mature eggs move to the outer edges of the ovaries and wait.

❖ The First Ovulation

At this point, the pituitary gland sends out a different hormone, called *luteinizing hormone* (LH). The LH causes *ovulation*—the release of one egg from an ovary. The egg is then caught and swept into the end of a thin tube, called a *Fallopian tube*. Slowly, the egg begins to travel down the tube toward the uterus, moved along by the contraction of tiny muscles on the tube's inside walls.

After the egg starts moving, the small sac that it was in begins to produce a hormone called *progesterone,* which tells the uterus to thicken its lining and prepare for the possibility that a fertilized egg will attach to its lining and begin to grow.

For pregnancy to occur, a male reproductive cell (sperm) must fertilize an egg. Sperm must enter the woman's body in order to fertilize an egg. How this happens is discussed on page 101.

If the egg isn't fertilized, it disintegrates when it reaches the uterus. The egg sac stops making progesterone. In response, the uterus releases the lining, which is what causes a period to begin.

At this point, hormone production has slowed way down. When the level of hormones in the bloodstream reaches a certain low point, the brain sends signals to the pituitary gland, telling it to send out more hormones to stimulate the release of another egg.

And the whole cycle begins again.

❀ You're Still Growing Up

BEFORE   AFTER

Beginning to menstruate is a major development toward becoming an adult woman— but only in the physical sense. When you start your period, someone might tell you, "You're a woman now!"

But you really won't be—not for a while.

You will still be a girl for a long time after you start your period. And you will still like to do the things you've always liked to do. And you'll still act the same way you've always acted. And your family will still love you in the same old way. And your parents will still boss you around.

The only difference is that for a few days each month, you will be wearing a pad or a tampon while you do things such as play soccer, paint your nails, eat root beer Popsicles, go to the mall, shout at your brother, talk on the phone, cheat against your best friend at Monopoly, and sit glassy-eyed on your bed staring at the TV and getting corn chip crumbs in the sheets.

Clues from Your Body

If you haven't started your period and you're wondering when you might, there's something that can at least give you a clue: your pubic hair.

Girls usually begin their periods sometime after they have quite a bit of pubic hair—not the fuzzy stuff that grows at first, but an actual bunch of hairs. They usually have some underarm hair, too.

In other words, don't expect to begin your period when your breast buds first appear or when you get your first few pubic hairs. Your breasts may develop and your pubic hair may begin to grow many months before you start your period.

What Does Menstruation Feel Like?

Menstruation feels as if you're leaking a small amount of liquid. You can't hold it back; the blood just comes out. But, remember, only a small amount is released at a time. You might notice it more when you change the position of your body—for example, when you stand up after you've been sitting down for a while.

When you urinate, it's easier for menstrual blood to come out of your vagina, so it does, often turning the toilet water pink. Sometimes you'll see small clots in the water and on the toilet paper after you've wiped yourself. This is normal.

The lining of your uterus comes off slowly over several days. Usually, most of it leaks out during the first few days of your period; then the flow gets lighter and lighter until there's nothing left but a few dribbles. But sometimes the flow is light at first, gets heavier, and then gets lighter again.

Odor

Menstrual blood has an odor when it hits the air. It's a natural smell, not at all unpleasant.

The smell can be strong, though. And when you sit down on the toilet, you may wonder if anyone else can smell this odor, which you may feel is private.

When a pad is snug against your body inside your underwear, the smell isn't at all noticeable to others. If you change your pad often enough—every three or four hours or so—and bathe regularly, nobody will notice it but you.

If you use tampons, the odor won't be noticeable, either (see pages 43–44).

BATHING

When you take a bath or shower, blood might come out in the water—and that's just fine.

cramps

During a period—usually at the beginning—some girls and women experience discomfort in the form of a dull ache or pain in the middle of the lower abdomen or in the lower back. This pain is usually referred to as *cramps*.

Cramps can make some people feel pretty rotten. Sometimes it may be necessary to ask your parent if you can take a mild pain reliever. *Do not take aspirin for cramps.* In rare cases, aspirin can cause a serious illness if a child or teenager takes it while infected with the virus that causes chicken pox or the flu. Since you have no way of knowing in advance if you are about to get sick, play it safe: *Don't take aspirin.*

There are over-the-counter medications that can help relieve cramps. Your doctor can recommend one.

Please don't take any drugs without asking permission first. Any drug can be harmful if you take too much of it, take it too often, or take it in combination with certain other medications. Read and follow all directions on the packaging.

Some girls and women find that a warm hot-water bottle resting on their abdomen makes them feel better when they have cramps. Lying in a comfortable position may also provide some relief.

When the Pain Doesn't Go Away

In some cases, girls and women have menstrual cramps that are so severe they need to see a doctor or other health care provider. A doctor can prescribe drugs that help manage the pain. No one needs to feel extreme pain when she's having her period.

Sometimes pain that occurs during menstruation actually is caused by something unrelated to your period. In other words, you are in pain, but menstruation isn't what's causing it. *Serious abdominal pain should always be reported to a doctor.*

Periods usually last three to seven days. Heavy flow for more than a week is unusual. Soaking a pad in less than an hour is unusual. You should see a doctor about any of these problems. Bleeding between periods should also be reported.

Women and girls with heavy periods need to be sure to eat foods that contain iron and to drink plenty of fluids. Sources of iron include leafy green vegetables, red meat, eggs, and fortified cereals or whole-grain cereals. Many girls take a multivitamin every day to make sure they are getting enough iron.

If you feel weak, dizzy, or faint with your periods, talk to a doctor.

Premenstrual Syndrome (PMS)

PMS stands for *premenstrual syndrome* and, among other things, it's about feeling grumpy before you begin your period each month.

Hormones are capable of causing extremely grouchy moods. Not all women and girls get grumpy and "out of sorts" before their periods begin, but plenty do. And many find things more upsetting than usual right before or on the first couple of days of their periods.

It's a good idea to keep track of when each of your periods begins by marking a calendar, in code if you want. That way, you can figure out how regularly or irregularly you menstruate. Sometimes your doctor will ask you if your periods are regular; if you have a marked calendar, you will know. And you may be able to predict and understand mood changes and physical changes that could be attributed to your menstrual cycle.

Some but not all girls have physical symptoms before their periods begin, such as tender breasts and puffiness in the hands, face, or abdomen.

Emotionally, PMS takes a variety of forms. It can include general irritability, door slamming, toothbrush throwing, desperate feelings about having nothing to wear, and arguments with friends at school.

Grown women can have PMS, too. It may account for the times your mom basically blows up just because every article of clothing you own has been thrown on your bedroom floor, along with nail polish, fish food, and pictures of cute guys torn out of magazines.

PMS hadn't been identified when I was a kid, but looking back, I remember thinking that my mother—who loved me—hated me. About once a month.

PMS is a nuisance! But it can be more than a nuisance; it can be a source of more serious physical and emotional upsets, and a number of women seek the help of health care professionals for PMS.

Chapter 3

Your Period—

How to Handle It

❀ A Misunderstanding

My friend Steven told me that when he was a kid, his job was to take out the trash and burn it in the incinerator in the backyard.

One day his older sister said, "Oh, Steven? By the way—don't bother burning the trash in the bathroom...I'll take care of that—from now on."

Steven was a very good boy, diligent about his chores.

And a very neat boy, apparently.

Because, at a later date, Steven noticed that the bathroom trash container seemed a little too full. So, what the heck! he decided. He might as well take it out and burn it himself.

To his surprise, Steven discovered...things... wrapped up in newspaper—scary things, in the bottom of the can. Upon close examination, Steven concluded the worst: They were big, fat bloody bandages.

He thought his sister had a mysterious bleeding disease! Brave as she was, Steven thought she had decided to keep this secret from the rest of the family.

And Steven honored her decision.

Steven was worried sick. But he was relieved to discover, over the months that followed, that his sister had long periods of recovery from her ailment: She needed bandages only intermittently, for a few days in a row, about, say, once a month.

Eventually, Steven's sister left home, went to college, got married, and had a family. Somehow, she had miraculously recovered! What a relief for Steven!

Out of concern for the environment, we no longer burn trash in backyard incinerators. Out of concern for kids, we no longer withhold information about periods. Most boys know what a "period" is. Still, questions come up as people grow up. Don't keep a troublesome secret. If anything confuses you, scares you, or makes you feel worried, talk to someone you trust.

✿ Preparing for Your First Period

Since no girl can tell exactly when her first period will begin, some mothers suggest that their daughters carry one wrapped pad in their purses or backpacks just in case. Your mom or stepmom or foster mom may begin tucking pads here and there, in your top drawer or your overnight bag. She may even buy whole boxes of pads and put them in your closet, whispering, "I know you don't need these yet, but just in case…"

When you begin your period for the first time, you will most likely notice it when you sit down to go to the bathroom. You'll see a spot of blood in your underwear. Or you might notice when you wipe that there's some rusty or pinkish color on the toilet paper.

If it first happens when you're at home, tell your mom or somebody else you feel comfortable talking to.

If nobody's home, don't worry—you can handle it. You'll know what's going on, and you'll know what to expect. If you feel a little anxious, that's okay.

If you have been given a "just in case" pad, get it. If you don't have a pad hidden away or if you cannot find it, but you know where your mom or sister stashes them, get one out. There's sticky stuff on the back of most pads, under a paper or plastic strip. Peel off the strip. Then stick the pad inside the crotch of your underwear. Remember: The pad is supposed to stick to your underwear—not to you.

Pull up your underwear and check to make sure the pad seems to be in the right position; just use your judgment and you won't be far off.

That's all you have to do.

Pads need changing every few hours. When you change a pad, don't flush it down the toilet, because it will plug up the plumbing. Roll it up, then wrap it in toilet paper or in the wrapper for your new pad, and put it in the trash.

❀**If** You Don't Have a Pad

If you don't have a pad, everything will be just fine. There are a lot of things you can use for a pad on a temporary basis. You can roll up some toilet paper around your hand—a bunch of it—and tuck it in your underwear. Or you can use a stack of tissues or paper napkins or paper towels and put it in your underwear, like a pad.

If there are no paper products available, help yourself to a clean, dry washcloth, fold it in half, and put it in your underwear. Blood washes out with cold water, so don't worry about ruining the washcloth. Or you can be inventive. Any small, absorbent, clean, washable piece of cloth or clothing can be used as a temporary pad—even a clean sock will do in a pinch.

You're Not at Home

If you're not at home when your period begins, don't worry. Most periods begin slowly, so you can just tuck something into your underwear temporarily to absorb the blood.

You probably won't have gotten any blood on your clothes when you first notice your period has begun. It will most likely be only in your underwear. But if a little has come through onto your pants, shorts, dress, or skirt, you can casually tie a sweatshirt or sweater around your waist, and nobody will know.

Try to get a pad as soon as you can, but there's no need to panic. If you're at school, and the bathroom doesn't have a pad vending machine, you may talk to a teacher or the school librarian, secretary, nurse, or principal; ask one of them to find a pad for you.

There are pads available in almost every school office because lots of girls begin their periods for the first time at school. Also, girls who have already started menstruating often have irregular periods that catch them by surprise. Remember: Almost all women who haven't reached menopause have periods. A female teacher might have a spare pad in her purse or in her classroom cupboard, which she would be happy to give to you.

Telling a friend might be a good idea. Friends have a way of being helpful and reassuring in these types of situations.

If you don't want to tell anyone except a family member, you can always resort to using toilet paper. If you want to, call a parent. If you need permission to make a call, just say it's for a reason that's private.

If you can't reach anyone, you can get through the day using toilet paper if you have to, even though you may have to reposition it and change it often.

❖ If *You Begin During the Night*

If you wake up and discover that you've begun your period during the night, you may have gotten a little blood in your pajamas or on your bedding, but nothing will have been ruined.

Blood can be washed out of clothing and bedding easily with cold water. Everything can wait until morning. Just put on a pad. Don't be afraid to wake up your mom and tell her if you want to. She can help you rinse your pajamas and bedding, but she'll probably wait until morning.

Almost every girl and woman has to wash menstrual blood out of underwear, clothes, or bedding sooner or later. It's actually easy. Wash the spot out with cold water and a little soap. Remember: Hot water turns the blood into a stain, but cold water, especially if you soak the garment for a few minutes, takes the blood out completely.

Once you've gotten the blood out of something that's washable, it can be washed along with the other laundry. But don't just throw it in the hamper when it's wet because wet stuff packed in a laundry basket or hamper can get moldy, especially in the summer. And mold stains are difficult, if not impossible, to get out. Instead, find a good place for it to dry before tossing it in with the other dirty clothes.

If you menstruate regularly, it's not a bad idea to wear a thin pad or a panty liner on days when you expect your period and to carry a pad in your purse or backpack.

✿ PADS

There are many kinds of pads made by a variety of companies, and they are available at grocery stores and drugstores. There are very big ones for wearing overnight, thin ones, contoured ones, long ones . . . New types seem to be invented regularly. Some have deodorant, some don't. Pads with deodorant may irritate sensitive skin, and they are not a substitute for changing your pad at regular intervals.

Panty liners are thin and not very absorbent; don't confuse them with regular pads. The purpose of a panty liner is, basically, to keep underwear "fresh." They're not effective as pads unless used at the end of your period, when the flow has just about stopped.

Almost all pads have a layer of plastic inside them to keep blood from leaking all the way through. Some have plastic gathers on the sides or wraparound sticky flaps (called "wings") to help keep blood off your underwear.

But, over the years, I have noticed that menstrual blood finds its way into underwear no matter what. Many girls and women don't wear their best underwear during the first few days of their periods.

❖ Tampons

A *tampon* is an alternate way of absorbing menstrual blood. It works like a soft plug that soaks up blood in the vagina, before the blood has a chance to dribble out. A tampon is inserted directly into the opening of the vagina, usually by way of a disposable applicator.

There's a string attached to a tampon. After the tampon is inserted, the string hangs out of the vagina so it can be pulled back out easily. If it's in right, it's comfortable.

When the tampon has absorbed all it can, or before four hours have passed, you pull it out by the string and, if necessary, put in another tampon.

You'll be happy to know that a tampon can't get lost up inside of you. The vaginal walls and bottom of the uterus (*cervix*) prevent it from traveling anywhere. Once it's inserted, you might think of a tampon as being inside a pouch. If the string somehow goes up into the pouch, you can find it by gently pushing one clean finger into your vagina, feeling for the tampon string or the tampon, and pulling it out.

After a tampon is removed, wrap it in toilet paper and put it into the trash. Or flush it down the toilet, unwrapped. If the applicator is flushable, it will say so on the packaging. If in doubt, wrap it up and throw it out.

Flushable tampons and flushable applicators can cause problems with the plumbing if a house has its own septic system. Find out whether or not you can flush tampons at your house.

Important Information About Tampons

It's a good idea to wait for several menstrual cycles before using tampons, because using a tampon can be tricky—and the *safe* use of tampons depends on knowing the basics about your menstrual flow. You might ask your doctor when he or she thinks it's okay for you to begin using tampons.

Most girls are puzzled at first about how to use tampons. You may want to ask your mom to explain or demonstrate.

There are detailed instructions on a folded-up piece of paper inside the box. Take the time to read them carefully—don't just skim them.

There's a warning in every box of tampons about an illness called *toxic shock syndrome (TSS)*. It's important to know about TSS before trying out tampons.

Toxic Shock Syndrome (TSS)

Toxic shock syndrome (TSS) is a very rare, but very serious, illness, in which bacterial toxins from the vagina enter a girl's or a woman's bloodstream and cause her to become extremely sick—she may even die. TSS sometimes can develop as a result of using tampons, particularly when they are used incorrectly. TSS can also develop from using certain types of contraception that involve placing a device (diaphragm or cervical cap) into the vagina, especially when left in longer than recommended (see page 147).

The symptoms of toxic shock syndrome include high fever, vomiting, diarrhea, lightheadedness, aching muscles, headaches, and—visible on light-skinned people—a rash that looks like sunburn. TSS begins and progresses quickly, but can usually be treated when the symptoms are noticed early.

If you have any of these symptoms while using a tampon, take it out and call a doctor immediately. Tell the doctor that you have been using tampons. If you have these symptoms while not using a tampon, still call the doctor; TSS can occasionally occur without a tampon having triggered it.

The Correct Use of Tampons

Tampons come in junior, regular, and super absorbencies. To be safest, girls and women should use the *least* absorbent tampon that works. If juniors work, use juniors. If juniors fill up too soon to be effective, use regulars. Super-absorbent tampons are more likely to play a part in triggering toxic shock syndrome than regular or junior tampons.

If juniors and regulars leak a little, you can wear a minipad or panty liner to catch the overflow.

On days of your period when the flow is light or spotty, don't use tampons, which may be dry and scratchy. Use pads instead.

Leaving tampons in too long can also help trigger toxic shock syndrome. Use pads at night while you sleep—not tampons.

On days when you use tampons, change them regularly: every three to four hours.

Inserting Tampons

The opening of the vagina, in most girls, is covered partially by the hymen. Occasionally, the structure of the hymen will not allow easy passage of a tampon. Usually, though, the hymen will allow insertion of a tampon, particularly a slender one.

Wash your hands before putting in a tampon so that the applicator will be as clean as possible.

Inserting a tampon should not be painful. If it hurts, stop.

You may need to ask your mom or big sister to coach.

✿ My First Tampon Experience

When I first started my period, tampons were available, but people didn't approve of young girls using them.

I didn't even know they existed!

The pre-tampon summer crowd always included some poor girl (like me, for example) who sat roasting by the pool or on the beach because she "couldn't swim." (The great big pads we used to wear were detected easily in a bathing suit.)

We had to lie to younger kids who didn't understand the meaning of the code words: "I can't swim." They'd hound us; they'd interrogate us. ("But I've seen you swim!") We'd make excuses like "Well... actually, today I just didn't feel like it."

Even though it may have been, say, ninety-five degrees in the shade.

To make matters worse, we had to worry about whether some playful boy (who had no older sisters to clue him in) was going to get funny and shove us into the water.

I think I was about fifteen when I discovered tampons and tried to put one in. First, I briefly skimmed the how-to diagram—a cross section of the lower half of a female standing sideways, which looked like a drawing of a lamb chop.

I discarded the instructions and carefully tore the wrong end of the paper wrapping off the applicator, causing the little cardboard tube to open in half and the tampon to fall out. I had to reload it, which was no small chore.

Little did I know that I would continue to make the same mistake on a regular basis for the next ten or twenty years of my life.

Next came the hard part: getting the tampon in. At that time, the tip of the applicators weren't rounded. Ouch! I poked and pushed, then gave up; it hurt too much!

After several rounds of this, I finally learned how to insert a tampon. The secret, I discovered, was to put it in at an angle, pointing it in the direction of my tailbone, instead of straight up.

I would have learned this by studying the lamb chop drawing more carefully.

Chapter 4

General Health —Checkups, Counseling, and Crisis Hotlines

✿ Checkups

If you haven't had a checkup lately, now might be a good time to make an appointment to get one.

A checkup is different from a visit to the doctor for an earache or a sore throat. It's a special appointment during which a doctor (or other qualified health care provider) spends time looking at "the whole picture," such as your height, your weight, your vision, and whether all your immunizations are up to date. A physical checkup for a growing girl also includes checking her blood pressure and the general condition of her heart, lungs, and abdomen.

A checkup provides a good opportunity to talk with a doctor about changes that may be going on in your body. If you have questions, you can ask them and get answers. It is also a good time to talk with your doctor about problems you may be having at home, in school, or with friends.

As you grow older, physical examinations become more extensive. Eventually a doctor will do routine breast checks and pelvic exams, and will show you how to examine your own breasts so that when you grow up, you can be alert to breast cancer.

✿ *Pelvic Exams*

A *pelvic exam* is when a doctor checks a woman's or young woman's vagina, cervix, and other internal reproductive organs. When girls are young, a pelvic exam is done only if a problem is suspected and is not included in a routine checkup.

Teenagers who are sexually active should schedule routine pelvic exams. These exams are usually done in a gynecologist's office. Women should have routine pelvic exams, whether or not they are sexually active. At what age should a young woman begin to schedule pelvic exams and breast checks? Ask your doctor.

✿ Scoliosis Checks

Sometimes, as a young person begins to enter puberty, the spine grows a little faster than it should, and it begins to curve. This is called *scoliosis,* and in most cases, the problems associated with it can be avoided if a doctor becomes aware of it early. Scoliosis is one of many important reasons to have routine physical checkups.

Many school districts have programs in which the school nurse checks kids for scoliosis. Having your back checked for scoliosis doesn't hurt at all.

Eye Exams

A brief eye test (reading an eye chart) is part of a routine checkup. Your school may also offer eye testing. If not, be sure to tell your parents if you have trouble seeing the chalkboard at school, if movies seem blurry, or if it's difficult to read books and magazines.

If you need glasses, frames are available in many styles at a wide variety of prices.

If you are interested in contact lenses, listen care-

fully to what your eye doctor has to say about them. Leave contacts in only for the recommended length of time. Also, follow all instructions on cleaning your contacts. This is really important to help prevent eye infections and injuries.

*D*ental E*X* A M S

Dentists recommend that kids have dental checkups twice a year. Regardless of how often you go to the dentist, remember that brushing and flossing *do* make a difference; brush as soon as you can after every meal. Use fluoride toothpaste, especially if your water is not fluoridated.

Chewing sugarless gum helps flush the teeth with saliva and may help prevent cavities, but brushing is better.

❉ Orthodontic Exams

A dentist may recommend that you make an appointment with an *orthodontist*. An orthodontist is a dentist who corrects irregularities of the bite. The orthodontist will evaluate whether or not you need braces.

Not every family can afford braces. However, it's usually possible to straighten your teeth or improve your bite when you're an adult, if you still want to by the time you grow up.

Acne

Many girls (and boys) get acne—otherwise known as blemishes, pimples, and "zits"—when they begin to go through puberty. Sometimes acne persists throughout the teens and into the twenties. For a rare few, including me, zits continue to blossom into middle age—usually on the eve of an important social event.

Luckily, there are products that actually work to minimize the problem. You can ask a pharmacist about nonprescription acne medications, including soaps.

Your doctor may prescribe medication for your acne or may suggest a medication that is available without a prescription. Or he or she may refer you to a *dermatologist*. A dermatologist is a doctor who specializes in the care of skin.

Keeping your skin clean is a good idea. It's especially important to wash your face if you wear makeup. Beware of perfumed soaps, which may aggravate the problem.

Unless you have a specific allergy, snack foods—including chocolate and chips—do *not* cause acne. But eating well does contribute to good health in general, including the health of your skin. Eat a balanced diet of fresh fruits and vegetables, whole grains, lean meat, fish, poultry, eggs, and dairy products. Snack foods, in moderation, are fine, too.

❖ FOOD
and YOUR HEALTH

Everyone's body needs food to perform properly. A healthy diet includes appropriate combinations of proteins, fats, carbohydrates, and all of the vitamins and minerals required by the body. A well-balanced diet can be achieved by eating a good selection of fruits and vegetables, low-fat dairy products, whole-grain cereals and breads, and lean red meat, chicken, and fish.

Those who choose to eat a vegetarian diet must be extra careful to meet their nutritional needs. This is especially important for kids who are growing. Before deciding to eliminate meat and/or dairy from your diet, consult a health care professional.

Try not to skip meals.

Kids who don't eat breakfast don't perform as well as they could in school. If you skip breakfast, it means that your body has had to go all night and then all the next morning until lunch to get the nourishment it needs. This can make you feel weak, irritable, sick, down in the dumps—and not interested in your schoolwork.

At least eat a bowl of cereal in the morning. And

A Shopping List of Nutritious, Low-Fat Foods

Fruits and Vegetables and Legumes

Apples
Apricots
Bananas
Bok choy
Broccoli
Brussels sprouts
Cabbage
Cantaloupe
Carrots
Cauliflower
Chickpeas

Dried beans (navy
    beans, pinto
    beans, black
    beans, etc.)
Grapefruit
Greens
Kale
Melons
Oranges
Peaches
Pears

Potatoes
Prunes
Raisins
Raspberries
Red and green
    peppers
Spinach
Strawberries
Sweet potatoes
Tomatoes
Winter squash

Animal Products

Cheese (made from skim milk)
Chicken/turkey (remove skin)
Fish
Lean meats (trim fat)
Milk (nonfat/low fat)
Yogurt (nonfat/low fat)

Cereals and Grains

Brown rice
Corn tortillas
Pasta
Whole-grain bread
Whole-grain cereals

Source: American Cancer Society.

grab a banana or an apple on your way out the door!

Do you like drinking milk? If not, eat yogurt or cottage cheese. Your bones and teeth are still growing, and you need lots of calcium, which is found in milk products, to help make that happen.

Focusing on Appearance

There are good reasons to eat a nutritious, low-fat diet and to exercise regularly. These things promote fitness. It's appropriate to have goals of being healthy, strong, and in good shape.

Focusing on appearance is a natural part of growing up. But TV, movies, and ads often portray unrealistic images of women. The influence of the media can have a harmful effect—especially on teenage girls.

People are genetically programmed to be a variety of sizes and shapes. Accept your body type. It's true that we can all live without that second piece of cake or pie, or that extra scoop of ice cream, but don't diet, unless you are being supervised by a medical doctor who has recommended a specific nutritional program.

❀ Eating Disorders

Some girls and women become very, *very* preoccupied with trying to be thin. This preoccupation may be a symptom of an *eating disorder*. An eating disorder is an illness that causes someone to purposely starve, exercise too much, abuse laxatives, or make himself or herself throw up to lose weight or to avoid gaining weight.

Anorexia nervosa is a condition in which a person restricts food intake too much and falls below his or her ideal body weight range. *Bulimia* is a condition in which a person regularly binges on food, then starves or uses laxatives or vomiting to avoid putting on weight. Often a person with an eating disorder does not recognize or admit that he or she has this problem.

Anorexia and bulimia pose very serious health risks. Many girls die of eating disorders every year. But with help from health care professionals, it is possible to overcome an eating disorder. Questions or concerns about yourself or a friend? Talk to a parent, doctor, teacher, or counselor.

✿ Counseling

Everybody experiences feelings of sadness, loneliness, and confusion at one time or another. Changes in feelings or moods are a perfectly natural part of growing up. Sharing your feelings—happy and sad—with those whom you trust and love builds strong, healthy relationships.

Not all troublesome feelings or conflicts can be resolved by talking about them with your family and friends. If you are troubled by sad, worried, or anxious feelings that don't go away or keep coming back again, ask for help. If your emotions seem out of control, ask for help.

You can get help by asking your parents, doctor, teacher, or school counselor—or another adult you trust—to help you find a psychologist, psychiatrist, or counselor. Or you can call the *county health department* for a referral. (Ask the information operator [411] or look under "county government" listings in the phone book.) Or you can call a youth crisis hotline (see page 64).

It's perfectly all right to call 911 or the police emergency number in any health emergency, including a mental health emergency.

Therapy

Doctors and other adults are aware of the stress that can accompany growing up, and every community has mental health care available for children. Mental health care may include medication and/or *therapy*.

Therapy is a process that involves talking and listening. With guidance from a trained health care provider, we can explore and identify what is making us feel bad and work through the problem. As the problem is resolved, positive thoughts and good feelings may replace the negative, sad ones.

It isn't necessary to feel sad, scared, anxious, or "out of control" to get counseling help. Lots of people talk to mental health care professionals to gain insight and improve coping skills. Getting therapy doesn't mean you're crazy or can't help yourself. It enables you to understand your life better and feel more in control of it.

DRUGS, *Alcohol*, and Stress

Some people may use illegal drugs or alcohol to try to manage stress or other uncomfortable or painful feelings. While some of these substances may *seem* to offer temporary relief, they're actually harmful to emotional well-being and physical health (see pages 65–77).

Suicide Threats

If anyone talks to you about wanting to end his or her own life, tell a parent, teacher, the school principal, counselor, a health care professional, a police officer, or another adult you trust. Tell right away, even if you promised you wouldn't. Don't try to decide whether or not the person might actually attempt suicide—all threats of suicide must be taken seriously. Remember: In any emergency, call 911 or the police emergency number.

Also—there are suicide prevention and youth crisis hotlines available. The numbers can be found by calling the information operator. The Boys Town National Hotline is also a suicide prevention hotline: 1-800-448-3000 (see page 64).

YOUTH CRISIS HOTLINES

Youth crisis hotlines are staffed by trained volunteers or professional counselors who help callers identify their problems, explore options, and develop a plan of action. They also offer referrals to community-based services, support groups, and even shelters, if necessary. You will find hotline numbers on page 64.

Sometimes hotline numbers change.

The front pages of the phone book often list hotline numbers along with other emergency numbers. Or you can call the information operator (411) or the regular operator (0) and ask for help in finding a hotline number that you need.

✿ Running Away

Some kids experience situations such as abuse, a serious breakdown in communication with parents, conflicts within the family, or other stressful circumstances that make them feel as if they just can't cope if they remain at home.

Running away to the streets is not a solution; it

exposes kids to crime and violence, hunger, disease, and to people who prey on kids. All kids need to be under the care and supervision of a responsible adult.

Most problems *can* be solved by remaining at home; there are thousands of agencies and support groups set up to help kids and their families find safe solutions to problems by taking advantage of services (like family counseling) within their own communities.

These agencies and groups can be found by asking people—such as a school counselor, teacher, principal, or health care professional. They can be found by looking in the phone book under "government" listings (turn to "county government" and look under "health services" and "social services") or by asking the information operator (411) for government "social services" listings. Or, they can be found by getting a referral from a youth crisis hotline (see page 64).

Sometimes, it is in the kid's best interest for alternate living arrangements to be made, either on a temporary or permanent basis. These arrangements need to be made by responsible adults who are in a position to safeguard a child's health and welfare.

Social service agencies run by the government are equipped to handle these arrangements.

In any emergency, including a mental health emergency, call 911 or the police emergency number for your area, or dial "0" and ask the operator for help.

THE FOLLOWING HOTLINES ARE CURRENTLY AVAILABLE FOR ANYONE TO CALL, FREE, 24 HOURS A DAY:

Covenant House Nine Line (youth crisis line— to talk about *any* problem): **1-800-999-9999 (U.S. only)**

National Runaway Switchboard (youth crisis line—for kids who are thinking about running away, for kids who have already run away, or for kids who want to talk about other problems):
1-800-621-4000 (U.S. only)
For the hearing impaired: **1-800-621-0394 (TTY)**

• **Child Help IOF Forester's National Child Abuse Hotline** (if there are concerns about physical, sexual, or emotional abuse or neglect): **1-800-4-A-CHILD   (1-800-422-4453) (U.S. and Canada).** For the hearing impaired: **1-800-2-A-CHILD (1-800-222-4453) (TTY)**

Boys Town National Hotline (youth crisis line—to talk about *any* problem): **1-800-448-3000 (U.S. and Canada)**
For the hearing impaired: **1-800-448-1833 (TTY)**

The above hotline calls are free. Anyone can call, and the call doesn't appear on the phone bill. It may be necessary to wait for a few moments for a counselor to come on the line.

Chapter 5

DRINKING,

Smoking, *and*

Doing Drugs

Tobacco, Alcohol, and Other Drugs

Now that you're getting older, you may hear about or know kids who are experimenting with tobacco, alcohol, or drugs. Know the facts about these substances so that you can avoid the problems associated with their use.

✿ The Effects of Alcohol

When a person drinks an alcoholic drink, such as beer, wine, or hard liquor, the alcohol is absorbed into the bloodstream through the stomach and intestines. Since alcohol doesn't need to be broken down to be absorbed like other foods, it enters the bloodstream quickly—within five or ten minutes.

Alcohol circulates throughout the body. It circulates through the brain, where it initially causes a sense of well-being. It can also cause feelings of great self-confidence, insight, and ability. In reality, though, alcohol diminishes ability: it dulls awareness, slows

65

reflexes, impairs judgment, and interferes with physical coordination.

The more alcohol a person drinks, the more profound the effects are on the brain and other systems of the body. Drinking alcohol can cause a person to become confused, to stumble, to have slurred speech, to vomit, and to lose consciousness (pass out). Drinking too much alcohol can result in *alcohol poisoning*.

Alcohol Poisoning

Drinking too much alcohol can become a medical emergency. Too much alcohol can cause the brain to stop giving out signals telling the lungs to breathe. Without oxygen, the heart cannot beat—and a person can die simply because he or she has drunk too much. Too much alcohol can cause someone to pass out or fail to wake up or be woken up. A person who has passed out may throw up while asleep, and choke on the vomit. If you suspect alcohol poisoning, or believe that a drunk person's safety is otherwise in jeopardy, get help from a sober, responsible adult *without delay*. Or call 911 (or the police emergency number). Don't worry about whether or not somebody will get into trouble because of under-age drinking. Just get help!

Why Do People Drink Alcohol?

Adults who drink alcohol usually drink it to relax, often in a social setting. After having a drink or two, a person may become talkative, may "loosen up."

Although people may feel "high" while drinking, alcohol is a *depressant* (it slows the body's systems down). And many people experience feelings of "being down" after the initial effects of alcohol have worn off.

Responsible drinkers are aware of the effects that alcohol can have on their systems. They know their limits and stay within them. But drinking responsibly not only involves knowing *how much* to drink. It also involves knowing *when*, *where*, and *with whom* it is safe to drink. Managing the effects of alcohol can be tricky, and that's why the legal drinking age is twenty-one in nearly all states.

Impaired Judgment and Alcohol

A person who is under the influence of alcohol has impaired judgment. He or she may make bad decisions or take dangerous risks, like driving a car or riding with a drunk driver or going off someplace with someone he or she doesn't know well enough to trust.

67

Bad judgment can also come into play regarding sex. Alcohol affects people's moods. Under the influence of alcohol, people may have romantic feelings or sexual urges that they act on which they normally wouldn't—and later regret. Also, they may decide to have sex without regard for the risk of pregnancy or the spread of sexually transmitted diseases. HIV is often spread when people who have been drinking take a chance and have sex without a latex condom (see page 125).

It's also possible for certain people to become aggressive when drinking, and this can lead to violence—including date rape and other kinds of sexual assault. A person under the influence of alcohol is an easy target for being harmed because he or she is physically and emotionally vulnerable.

SAY NO to Driving with Someone Who's Been Drinking

A person who has been drinking may reassure you that he or she can drive "just fine," but one of the effects of drinking alcohol is a false sense of confidence. If anybody who has been drinking offers to drive you somewhere, say no.

> *Alcohol interferes with reflexes and judgment long before a person is visibly drunk.*
>
> **What if he or she has drunk just a little bit?**
>
> A kid is not equipped to judge whether or not another person is okay to drive; call your parent or another responsible driver you trust if you find yourself in a situation in which an adult or teen who is in charge of your transportation has been drinking alcohol.

TOBACCO

Tobacco can be used legally by anyone over age eighteen. It is available in the form of cigarettes and cigars; loose tobacco comes in packages for pipes or for rolling into cigarettes. Smokeless (chewing) tobacco comes in small cans. Some teenagers first try smoking cigarettes or chewing tobacco because they're curious. It's easy to get hooked—and it's hard to quit.

A substance present in tobacco called *nicotine* is addictive. Once people have used tobacco for a while, they feel compelled to smoke. During the course of the day, at intervals, a person gets a craving—a strong yearning for a cigarette. Also, reaching for a cigarette can become an automatic response to certain situations that include feeling worried, upset, nervous, anxious, or excited.

Long-term tobacco use causes heart disease, cancer, and respiratory illness and contributes to other serious health problems. Secondhand smoke from someone else's cigarette can be harmful to those who breathe it.

The tobacco industry uses advertising to try to recruit new tobacco users—for example, you!

Smoking doesn't have anything to do with beauty, sex, popularity, power, confidence, or success. Don't be fooled by the tobacco industry's ads—they just want you to get addicted to tobacco so they can make money selling cigarettes to you!

DRUGS

A drug is a chemical substance. Used correctly, some drugs prevent, treat, control, or cure disease. Others help people manage pain. Drugs can treat mental conditions, such as depression, or physical conditions, such as hay fever.

Legal drugs (medicines) include *over-the-counter drugs*, such as ibuprofen, and *prescription drugs*, such as antibiotics, which a pharmacist fills according to a doctor's request.

Illegal drugs include substances such as heroin, cocaine, "speed," LSD, and many others.

Sometimes legal drugs are used illegally—such as when a person uses a prescription drug for a different purpose than what was intended when it was prescribed.

Over-the-Counter Drugs

Over-the-counter drugs don't require a doctor's prescription, but they do require responsible, careful use. Ask your parents' permission before taking an over-the-counter drug, like a cough medicine, for example. Read the entire label, including the warnings, and

Don't take, or give anyone, medicine in the dark or when you're sleepy. If you need medicine in the middle of the night, wake up a parent and ask for help getting out the correct medicine and taking it.

check the recommended dose. Don't combine drugs without checking with the pharmacist or your doctor first. Combining drugs, including over-the-counter drugs, can be dangerous.

Prescription DRUGS

Containers that hold prescription drugs sometimes look alike. Before you take any prescription medicine, make sure it has your name on it, that it's the right medicine, that you know the correct amount to take, and that you're taking it for the reason for which it was prescribed.

> Never share medicine with a friend, including acne medicine and birth control pills.

Your doctor should be aware of all medications you are taking before prescribing additional drugs.

Illegal Drugs

Heroin, crack cocaine, cocaine, "crank" (speed), LSD (acid), and "designer" drugs such as "ecstasy" are examples of illegal drugs that are used by people who want to alter the way they feel. Drugs may seem to provide a temporary escape from reality and responsibility, tension, anxiety, or boredom. But the feelings that drugs produce are unpredictable, and don't necessarily provide this escape. And if they do provide it, it's just an illusion. The drug wears off, and the person experiences a letdown. Plus, the person's problems remain unresolved.

If the drug is addictive, the person will feel a need to take the drug again. The impulse to take the drug again can be so strong that the person will take it even though he or she knows it's damaging. Some people turn to crime, including prostitution, to get money to buy the drug to which they are addicted. Many people end up in jail as the result of drug addiction.

Some drugs cause permanent damage to the heart; others cause brain damage. Certain drugs cause people to become violent or suicidal.

A lot of teenagers are very curious about drugs and are tempted to experiment. But experimentation can lead to abuse, addiction, and emotional and physical harm.

Impaired Judgment and Drugs

Like alcohol, drugs can impair judgment and make people less likely to think about consequences and therefore less likely to protect themselves (and others) against dangerous situations, including exposure to HIV (see pages 131-143).

Different Types of Illegal Drugs

Some illegal drugs are swallowed, some are smoked, some are snorted up the nose. Others are injected with needles (called "shooting up"). Shooting drugs into a vein can lead to drug overdose and death. Sharing the equipment used to shoot up drugs, including steroids, can spread HIV (see pages 133–138) and other diseases.

Stimulants (uppers) make people feel "fired up" or "wired."

Depressants (downers) make people feel "slowed down."

Hallucinogens alter perception of space and time, and cause people to see and hear things that aren't real.

Steroids are used illegally by some people for the purpose of becoming more "buff" and/or improving their athletic performance. Abuse of steroids can cause dangerous mood swings, sexual dysfunction, and other problems.

MARIJUANA

People have been arguing for years about whether marijuana (weed, pot) is safe enough to be legalized. Regardless of the debate, marijuana should *not* be considered a harmless substance.

Marijuana smoke, like tobacco smoke, leaves a

residue in the lungs. Marijuana contains a mind-altering ingredient (THC), which can cause psychological problems for some people. Sometimes marijuana is "laced" with a more dangerous drug, which has an unexpected, devastating effect on the person smoking it.

Why Do People Do It?

Marijuana is usually rolled into a thin cigarette called a joint or smoked in a pipe. A few moments after the smoke is drawn into the lungs, it begins to take effect.

Some people like the way it makes them feel. Some feel relaxed; some feel they think better; and some just think it heightens their enjoyment of life. To them, the effects of smoking marijuana can seem positive at times. However, these feelings aren't consistent. Marijuana is also known to make people feel frightened, alienated, scared, lonely, or upset.

Some kids use marijuana because they want to do what their friends are doing—and not because the drug makes them feel good.

Another problem associated with the use of marijuana is that people begin to rely on it to escape from the challenging feelings they experience in everyday life. Frequent use of marijuana by teens interferes with the natural development of coping skills.

Also, marijuana is known to interfere with motivation and concentration—two essential ingredients to being a successful student.

Inhaling Chemical Fumes

Many products that can be purchased legally can be dangerous or deadly when misused. It's really risky and unhealthy to attempt to "get high" by inhaling the fumes of household products.

LEGAL CONSEQUENCES

The legal consequences of underage alcohol use and/or possession of alcohol and illegal substances vary from state to state. They can include having to spend time in juvenile hall, being placed on probation, being denied a driver's license until age 18, or having a driver's license suspended—even if no vehicle was involved.

Since driving under the influence of alcohol and illegal substances is so dangerous, penalties are severe, especially when a person is injured as a result

We **Learn** to deal with stress, frustration, anxiety, and other uncomfortable feelings. Those who use drugs to make stressful feelings go away don't confront the feelings and don't develop good strategies for dealing with life's challenges. As a result, teenagers who routinely use alcohol, marijuana, or other drugs can impair their development into strong and confident adults.

ANYONE WHO HAS A PROBLEM WITH DRUGS CAN GET HELP.

The National Council on Alcoholism and Drug Dependence Hope Line number is: **1-800-NCA-CALL (1-800-622-2255) (U.S. and Canada)** The call is free, confidential, and won't appear on the phone bill.

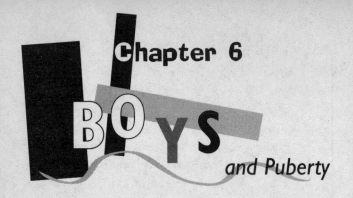

Chapter 6

BOYS and Puberty

The Camel Mask

When I was about nine or ten years old, our family had a great big music box with a large crank on the side. You could lift the lid, put on a big, flat tin circular "record," and listen to a hokey old tune—it was great! The problem was, my mom had let my brother have it in his room.

One afternoon, when my brother wasn't home, I decided to sneak into his room and listen to some music. A pile of clothing, books, and papers was on top of the music box. I carefully lifted off the objects, a few at a time, and stacked them on the rug.

Toward the bottom of the pile there was a rumpled-up sweater. I picked it up and...yikes! There was a horrible object under it! I jumped back. It was like discovering a fat white grub under a rotten log.

I examined it without touching it. It was made of

elastic; it looked like an Ace bandage with a knee pouch—or a surgical mask for a camel. It wasn't underpants, but it seemed like underpants. And it wasn't a bra, either—although it had a kind of bra-like look about it. Whatever it was, it wasn't supposed to see the light of day, so I quickly hid it again and tip-toed out of the room.

I wondered why my brother, whom I had former-ly admired, would have such an awful thing under a sweater on the music box—but I didn't dare ask why he had it or what it was.

I remember regarding him with suspicion for several days after seeing it—and I never tried to listen to the music box again, until it was safely moved out from underneath my brother's books, papers, and sweaters, out of his bedroom and into the den. Later, I learned that the camel mask was actually an athletic supporter. And I found out that there were other mysterious things going on with boys...

Boys and Puberty

As girls are busily cruising through the bra department and pondering boxes of maxipads in the grocery store, they may be asking themselves: What's going on with boys?

Like girls, boys have reproductive systems that

include internal and external sex organs. Their systems are also regulated by hormones, which signal for changes according to a boy's own individual timetable.

Boys, like girls, go through puberty. But, generally, they start the process a little later than girls do.

Physical Changes

Every boy is born with a *penis*. Unlike a vagina, a penis is hard to miss. A penis is a small, fleshy external sex organ found between a boy's legs. It is also an organ of excretion; urine leaves a boy's body through his penis.

Some boys are *circumcised* shortly after birth. This is surgery in which the *foreskin*, the fold of skin that covers the head of the penis, is removed.

When a boy goes through puberty, certain changes happen. His penis slowly begins to grow. His *testicles* (also called "balls") grow as well. Testicles are external sex organs that are located at the base of and underneath the penis. They look like two small eggs in a sac. The sac is called a *scrotum.*

Hairs sprout in a boy's armpits. They also grow at the base of his penis. After a while, he will have a triangular-shaped carpet of pubic hair. A boy can have curly or straight pubic hair, and it can be black, brown, blond, or red.

A boy begins to sweat more at puberty, and usually has the same concerns about underarm perspiration that a girl might. He may borrow a little deodorant from a family member, and then maybe buy his own.

If a boy doesn't already own an *athletic supporter* (also called a "jockstrap"), he might buy one now. An athletic supporter keeps his penis and testicles snug against his body when he plays sports.

During puberty, the hair on a boy's legs becomes thicker. His muscles begin to develop. He grows taller. Then his voice begins to change; it gets lower. He begins to grow more facial hair. He may grow hair on his chest.

Like many girls, a boy may worry about his body, wondering if he is growing and changing at the right rate. The bumps that precede pubic hairs may freak him out. He may worry about the length of his penis.

✿ FIND OUT YOUR FUTURE

Once I went to an accordion festival in the park and saw a woman advertising "psychic readings." She was sitting on a folding chair opposite another woman. Both had their eyes closed. Nearby was a sign: FIND OUT YOUR FUTURE: $5.

The "psychic" was mumbling to herself, wiggling her fingers in the air.

A boy about ten years old, standing next to his father, was watching carefully. As I passed by, I heard the boy whisper,

"Dad! Can you lend me five bucks? I want to find out how big my wiener's going to be when I grow up."

No one can predict how long a boy's penis will be when he grows up, but it doesn't take five dollars and a psychic to make a good guess. An adult male's penis is usually between two and five inches long; some are shorter, some are longer.

MORE ABOUT THE PENIS

At certain times, the penis can become erect, or temporarily bigger. When this happens, it's called having an *erection*.

Erections

Boys get erections from the time they are babies. Little boys often wake up with erections, and sometimes they get them when they have to urinate. This happens to older boys, too—and to men sometimes.

As boys get older (and go through puberty), they may get erections more often—even several times a day. Sometimes an erection happens when a boy thinks of or sees a person or a picture of a person he feels attracted to. This is referred to as becoming *sexually aroused* or "turned on"—or "excited."

Sometimes erections just happen for no apparent reason.

Usually, nobody notices, and a few minutes later, the boy's penis returns to its regular size.

Having an erection is sometimes called having a "boner" or a "woody," or "pitching a tent," or getting a "hard-on"—although these slang expressions aren't considered particularly polite. They're not accurate, either.

An erect penis isn't hard; it's just sort of solid as a result of being engorged with blood. And there's no bone in a penis, either.

An erect penis is usually about six inches long, but it can be longer or shorter and still be "the right size"—and still function as it's supposed to.

Testicles

Testicles are soft, sensitive, and vulnerable. And men and boys guard them from injury very carefully, because even a slight blow to the testicles hurts a lot. A blow to the testicles can bring a full-grown man to his knees.

While playing contact sports that pose a risk of injury to a boy's external sex organs, a boy needs to wear a "cup," which can be slipped into the pouch of an athletic supporter. A cup is made of plastic; it acts like a shell to protect the boy's penis and testicles in case they get hit by something, like a baseball.

Testicles also need to be protected because they have an extremely important function. *Sperm* (male reproductive cells) are made within the testicles. Without sperm, the human species would be unable to reproduce.

Why are testicles, which are such an important and sensitive male organ, located on the outside of the body, rather than on the inside?

The answer is this: Sperm must be produced at a temperature lower than that of the rest of the body. Since testicles hang down outside the body, they stay a little cooler.

SPERM

From puberty on, sperm are made inside a male's testicles around the clock, night and day, year in and year out. Sperm are so tiny that millions of them could fit in a teaspoon; they are so small that you can't see them without a microscope. Under a microscope, sperm look like mini tadpoles.

It takes many days for sperm to mature. As they do, they move through yards and yards of thin tubes wound up inside a man's testicles. They then pass into a storage place inside the male's body.

Preseminal Fluid

Preseminal fluid is a drop of fluid that appears at the tip of the penis when a male is sexually aroused. Preseminal fluid can contain a little bit of sperm. It may also contain germs that cause sexually transmitted diseases (see pages 131–143).

Seminal Fluid

Seminal fluid is a milky-colored liquid that is made in a small organ inside a male's body near where the sperm are stored. The function of seminal fluid is to energize the sperm and carry them along.

Semen and Ejaculation

At a point at which a male is highly aroused sexually, seminal fluid mixes with sperm, and this mixture, called *semen*, is pumped out of his body through his penis. This is called *ejaculation* (or "coming") and it's usually accompanied by a feeling of intense physical pleasure—known as an *orgasm*. Girls and women also experience orgasms, but in a different way (see pages 90–92).

Ejaculation has nothing to do with urinating. Making and storing urine in the body involves a separate set of organs. Even though semen and urine exit the body through the same tube in the penis, it's physically impossible for a man to urinate and ejaculate at the same time.

Wet Dreams

Sometimes, in the middle of the night, a boy will become sexually aroused and ejaculate while sleeping, getting his pajamas and bedding wet with semen. This is called having a *wet dream*. It's a natural occurrence and is nothing to worry about, although wet dreams might confuse or embarrass a boy who doesn't know what's going on. Wet dreams can happen throughout the life of a male.

Girls and women don't have wet dreams, but it's not unusual for a woman to experience an orgasm while sleeping (see page 91).

Chapter 7

Sex and Pregnancy

❖

The Birds and the Bees   Perhaps you've watched some of the nature programs on public television. Perhaps you've heard a commentator, maybe with an English accent, commenting on the "seggs-you-ality of the bub-boon" while two baboons show their gums to each other.

All living creatures reproduce—from the tiniest moth to the largest rhinoceros—and some of them reproduce sexually. To reproduce means to make anew; to make again. No species could continue to inhabit the earth without having the ability to reproduce.

When creatures reproduce sexually, it means that male and female parents each contribute *genes* to their offspring. Genes carry the information needed to form new life. They are contained in a female's egg and in the reproductive cells of a male and are united during the mating process.

Not all living things reproduce sexually, so not all living things have sex organs. Here are some that do: flowering plants, insects, reptiles, amphibians, fish, birds, and mammals.

Flowers have pretty little dusty sex organs. Bees help flowering plants mate by carrying their pollen from blossom to blossom. Apples, oranges, pears, peaches, and other fruits are the ripened ovaries of flowers.

Most species of animals can mate only with each other: bees with bees, birds with birds, goats with goats.

All of us who reproduce sexually have our own unique and mysterious ways of courting each other. These courtships result in the reproduction of our species.

✿ Sex

Sex is an instinctive attraction that draws us to others. Our sexuality develops as we grow from infancy to adulthood.

Sex is about exploring feelings that give pleasure. Sex can include touching our own bodies in ways that feel good.

Sex can be about intimate communication with another person to express love and affection. Sometimes this involves touching. When two people share sexual feelings by touching, each must have freely given permission to be touched.

In some cases, sex can include sexual intercourse, which can lead to a woman's becoming pregnant and having a baby. This is called *sexual reproduction*.

Exploring Your Own Sexual Response

When I was a kid, I didn't know what a *clitoris* was— at least I'd never heard or read the word.

I had discovered mine while bathing, but thought it was simply a cute little bump. I remember peering at it every once in a while, but I didn't know it had a function.

I don't recall touching it in ways that made me feel good, although I must have done this when I was a baby, since most girls do.

The best trick I knew for making myself feel good was sucking my thumb. I sucked my thumb and twirled my hair until I was twelve years old, and I enjoyed every minute of it, except when I'd been picking dandelions, which made my thumb taste bitter.

If I'd known about exploring my own sexual responses, I probably would have spent much less time lying in bed at night, staring blankly into the darkness, twirling my hair and sucking my thumb.

And my teeth would have ended up being straighter, too.

The clitoris is a little organ that every girl is born with. It's a small, sort of round bump located between the legs—just above the opening of the vagina. A clitoris is covered, or partly covered, by a hood of skin. If you look between your legs in private, you will find your clitoris. You may want to use a mirror to get a good look.

Stroking or rubbing the clitoris and the area around it can cause a girl to become sexually aroused. Most girls and women produce a slippery fluid in the vagina when they are sexually aroused. This is called *vaginal fluid*. Stroking and rubbing your clitoris in a way that gives pleasure is called *masturbation* (or "solo sex"). Masturbating can also include touching other private places on the body, including your breasts.

Sometimes masturbating can cause an orgasm. An orgasm is an amazing physical reaction. It's an extremely pleasurable sensation that starts between the legs and kind of washes over the body, all the way out to the ends of fingers and toes.

For most girls and women, having an orgasm takes patience and practice.

For people who feel okay about it, masturbating privately is a safe form of sexual exploration. It's a perfectly natural, healthy thing to do.

It's also perfectly natural not to masturbate—not all people want to.

Boys Masturbate, Too

Almost all boys who have reached puberty masturbate. A boy masturbates by touching his body in ways that cause pleasant physical sensations.

He may stroke, rub, and/or gently pull on his penis in a rhythmical way. This causes him to become sexually aroused. When aroused, he will have an erection. If he keeps on stroking and rubbing, he will ejaculate and have an orgasm.

Sometimes, a boy might worry that masturbating is unhealthy—that he might use up all of his sperm by masturbating. But sperm doesn't get used up; a boy's body will just keep on making more. And masturbating doesn't cause problems with eyesight or athletic abilities, as some people used to think. As long as a boy feels okay about doing it, masturbating privately is a safe way to explore his own sexual response.

🌸 *M*inor Details

Within a year of getting my first bra, I had a small lavender lace garter belt and beige seamed stockings. I had a gold metal razor and a green plastic box with razor blades. I had nicks on my legs and a rash under my arms from shaving. I had my own deodorant.

I had lavender lipstick and lavender nail polish.

But I didn't have the slightest clue that the changes that were happening to my body had anything to do with sexual reproduction. I didn't even know there was such a thing.

The closest I got to knowing anything about sexual reproduction was when I saw my cats mating. But I had no idea anything was going on beyond them looking stuck together in the marigolds.

If there were books about this topic for kids my age, I didn't know about them. Pamphlets were passed around—"girl talk" pamphlets—and I read one or two, but they were deliberately vague and sketchy. The pamphlets talked about breasts, pubic hair, and beginning to menstruate. They would mention pregnancy—telling about the uterus and the teeny embryo growing in it, and how it would develop into a fetus and then a baby.

The pregnancy section would always begin something like this: "After the egg is fertilized, it begins to grow inside the body of the mother…"

The pamphlet would leave out what the "fertilizer" was and where it came from. These "minor details" would be left out as if they weren't the least bit important, and not worth mentioning.

The strategy of parents in the 1950s was to withhold all facts about sex from kids until the kids got old enough to be so embarrassed by the topic that they would refuse to talk about it.

When somebody's mom got pregnant, she would

EXACTLY HOW DID THIS HAPPEN?!

BABY ON BOARD

be the last person to admit having had sex with her husband.

The pregnant mom would play dumb. Yes, a baby was magically growing in "her stomach"; there was no explanation offered as to why or how it had gotten there. Questions such as "When you eat, how come food doesn't fall on top of the baby's head?" were answered by vague gestures meaning "Who knows?" (or "Don't ask.").

More assertive lines of questioning—such as "Exactly how did you end up pregnant, anyway?"—were evaded by:

- ✿ Developing temporary hearing loss
- ✿ Counterattacking with an unrelated question ("Who borrowed my red nail polish and left the lid off?")
- ✿ Changing the subject ("Why don't you girls make a fort upstairs with a card table and blankets?")
- ✿ Making a quick exit ("Oops! I forgot all about the angel food cake in the oven!")

✿ The Co-conspirators

There was no reason for the average kid to suspect the involvement of a man in his wife's pregnancy.

In most families, the father went off to work in the morning carrying his lunchbox or briefcase, and arrived home at suppertime. After nine months of acting like an innocent bystander, he would begin to participate in the pregnancy by doing things like helping the mother-to-be put on and tie her shoes.

When the woman was ready to have the baby, the father's main job was to be prepared and drive her to the hospital. Typically, or so the story went, the trip would include driving the car in a rainstorm or snowstorm at three o'clock in the morning—the gas gauge on empty and the overnight bag for the mother-to-be left sitting at home by the front door. After the baby was born, this part of the story, which seemed like an episode from *I Love Lucy*, would be told again and again.

What we did not know was how the baby was born. Since we were unaware that the female anatomy included a vagina, we assumed the obvious: The baby squeezed out of the stomach through the only respectable hole below the waist on the human body—the belly button.

In the weeks and months that followed, the father would briefly hold the baby when it was in a good mood. But since caring for babies was considered "women's work," he would pay little attention to the child until it was safely out of diapers, eating solid foods, and able to walk on its own—preferably carrying a fishing pole and a jar of worms.

❂ Revelations

Somewhere along the way, certain kids would accidentally stumble upon information about sexual reproduction in books left carelessly around in places such as under the pajamas in the bottom of an older sister's dresser drawers. If the information leaked within the family and reached the mother, she would instruct her daughter *not* to tell any of her friends about it, since it was up to their own parents to tell them.

Naturally, girls then—as now—were interested in nosing around to find out who else might know. Inquiries would go something like this:

Girl #1: "Do you know about the birds and the bees?"

Girl #2: "Huh?"

Girl #1: "Grow up."

Or Girl #1 might motion you aside and tell you a joke in a low voice, stopping for a minute if somebody else passed by. She would say the punch line, and you would look at her, mystified, and say something like: "What do you mean, 'an elephant with an election'?"

She'd make a face and walk away. So you would repeat the joke at home, hoping for an explanation or maybe a good laugh at the dinner table.

Your parents would suddenly go silent. After a pause and a mouthful or two of mashed potatoes, your father would ask, in a serious voice, "Is there any more gravy?"

Later, when you were alone with your mother, drying dishes, she would casually say, "So, who told you the joke?"

For some reason, you would suddenly get amnesia.

Sooner or later, someone would just plain flat out tell you what people did to make a baby: The man puts his you-know-what into the woman's you-know-what.

what?!?!

This would be a shocking bit of news, even for someone who didn't have the slightest idea what the woman's you-know-what could be. And the response would be almost universal: You have *got* to be kidding!

That would usually be the end of the conversation—at least until you got together with your cousins. Getting together with cousins on holidays would often include heated debates about human reproductive activity—that is, sexual intercourse—while the grown-ups, disgusting as they seemed, were downstairs eating liver pâté on crackers, playing innocent.

These people, these so-called adults, must have had sexual intercourse more than once—once, in fact, for every baby they had. The notion that parents could have done it two or three times was…staggering.

The idea that adults would want to have sex for the fun of it, without even wanting or planning to have a baby, simply never crossed our minds.

✿ What Happens During Intercourse Between a Man and a Woman

When a man is sexually aroused and about to have sexual intercourse with a woman, his penis is erect. An erect penis points straight out or up. This makes it possible for him to guide it carefully into the woman's vagina.

Under most circumstances, the woman, like the man, becomes sexually aroused during the sexual activity that usually precedes the act of intercourse: undressing, hugging, kissing, and touching private places.

When a woman is sexually aroused, she produces extra vaginal fluid that makes it easier for the man's penis to enter her vagina.

After moving his penis in and out in a rhythmical way, the man ejaculates. The semen travels out of his body through his penis and is deposited inside the woman's vagina.

Having sexual intercourse (also called "making love") is usually accompanied by strong, pleasurable emotional and physical sensations for both the man and the woman.

When people become sexual partners, they can teach each other what feels good so that the experience of having sex together is satisfying for both; usually, it takes practice for both partners to have an orgasm during sexual intercourse.

Sexual intercourse can lead to a woman's becoming pregnant. However, the purpose of sexual intercourse isn't always to make a baby. People who want to have intercourse but do not wish to create a baby, use birth control (see pages 144–156).

✿ How Does Sexual Intercourse Make a Baby?

After sexual intercourse, the sperm that have been deposited in the vagina travel through an opening in the cervix, called the *os*. Each sperm has something that looks like a tail, and a sperm can move forward by wiggling it—as a tadpole does.

If there's an egg at the right spot in one of the Fallopian tubes, one sperm finds it and gets inside. This event is called *fertilization* of the egg, or *conception*. As soon as one sperm gets in, all the others are shut out.

Alternative Insemination

In some cases, a woman wants to have a baby—but she doesn't have a male partner, or her partner's sperm don't "work" to fertilize the egg. Sperm from a fertile male are introduced into the body of the woman, usually under the supervision of a health care professional. This is called alternative insemination. By using *alternative insemination*, pregnancy can occur without sexual intercourse. Lots of babies are conceived this way!

Pregnancy

As soon as an egg is fertilized, it begins to grow by a process called *cell division*. The fertilized egg—at first, one cell—divides, then divides again, and again. This process continues as the fertilized egg moves down the Fallopian tube and implants itself in the lining of the wall of the uterus.

After the egg is in place, the outer cells of the egg organize to form an organ called the *placenta*. The placenta surrounds the fertilized egg (now called an *embryo*) and grows along with it.

The placenta also produces a pregnancy hormone that causes changes in the mother's body that are needed to support a pregnancy. These changes include further development of the placenta and uterus, changes in the milk-producing glands in preparation for breast-feeding after the baby is born, and other changes that maintain a healthy environment as the embryo continues to grow.

In the first few weeks of the development of an embryo, the basic systems of its body are formed. When the embryo's body structures are in recognizable human shape (at eight weeks), it is called a *fetus*.

The placenta provides nourishment to the developing fetus and eliminates its waste products. It also acts as a filter between the mother and the fetus, keeping their blood separated. It allows nutrients and dissolved oxygen to enter the fetus's bloodstream. The fetus is attached to the placenta by the umbilical cord.

The placenta screens out things that the fetus doesn't need, or that may be harmful. It is not a perfect filter, however, and most drugs, including alcohol, can pass through it and into the fetus's bloodstream, causing harm. To protect her developing child, a pregnant woman should not smoke or take any drugs, including alcohol, unless prescribed by her doctor.

The fetus's life is entirely supported by its mother's body. It is important for the mother-to-be to eat a balanced diet to stay strong and healthy, because the physical development of the fetus is dependent on the mother's being well nourished.

At about four months, the mother can feel the fetus moving inside her. It feels like a flutter—like a butterfly flapping its wings.

By seven months, a fetus has a pretty good chance of surviving outside of its mother's uterus—although babies born this early usually require intensive medical support.

After nine months have passed, the baby is ready to be born.

Nobody knows exactly what triggers the onset of

the baby's passage from the mother's uterus into the outside world (called *labor*). But when the time comes, the muscles of the uterus begin to contract and these contractions cause the cervix to open up. This usually happens very slowly, over a period of many hours.

Once the cervix is all the way open, it becomes time for the mother-to-be to push down as hard as she can with her belly muscles, along with each contraction. This moves the baby out through the vagina.

The baby's head stretches the walls of the vagina and makes way for the rest of the baby's body to fit out of the vaginal opening. The process of labor usually takes between eight and twenty-six hours for a first baby, but the "pushing out" and delivery of the baby happens quite quickly at the end of the labor.

Labor can be very painful, but most mothers agree that the memory of the pain starts to fade shortly after her baby is born.

✿ If You Have Any Questions, Just Ask

Several months after I got the "you-know-whats" scoop from a friend and told every other girl my age who didn't already know, my mother announced that my best friend, Peg, and her mother were coming over for a visit.

At about four o'clock, they showed up. Before Peg and I had a chance to go into my room and wonder out loud why our moms were whispering, my mother called us into the living room where she and Peg's mom were sitting, each holding a cup of tea.

"Girls," said my mother. "It's time you knew the facts of life."

Peg's mother looked into her teacup.

"Everything reproduces," said my mother. "The birds, the bees. Everything."

Peg's mother kept looking at her tea.

"People reproduce, too," continued my mother. "And to reproduce, the man puts his penis into the vagina."

Peg and I just sat there, afraid to look at each other.

"Any questions?" asked my mother.

We shook our heads no.

"Well, if you have any questions, just ask," said my mother. "Either of you can ask either of us any questions, whenever you want, about anything."

Peg and I stood up, made abrupt about-faces, and hurried out of the room.

"You never told me *bees* did it!" Peg said when we were safely in my bedroom with the door shut. "How do you suppose bees do it?"

I didn't know. I didn't know how birds did it, either.

I still don't.

Chapter 8

Crushes, Kisses, and Other Matters

❀ Crushes

As your own sexual feelings emerge, you may find yourself very attracted to certain people, such as movie stars or musicians or other celebrities.

You may also have crushes on people you know, such as teachers!

When a kid gets a crush on a singer or a movie star, or a cute teacher, the kid may imagine what it might be like to be with that person romantically.

Having romantic fantasies (pretending in your mind) is a safe way for a kid to imagine being in a sexual situation *without actually being in one*.

It's never safe or okay for a kid to actually be in a sexual situation with an adult (see page 162).

Crushes on Relatives

You may also be surprised by sexual feelings toward your relatives, of either sex.

Getting a crush on a relative is very common. While it's perfectly natural to feel attracted to a family member, it's not okay to act on these feelings in a sexual way. Having sexual feelings and fantasies is completely different from *acting on* those feelings and thoughts (see page 167).

✿ **SEXUAL ORIENTATION**

The words *sexual orientation* describe whether a person is attracted to people of the opposite sex, people of the same sex, or people of both sexes. The concept of how people get their sexual orientation is not fully understood. Some people believe that our sexual orientation is something we are born with. Others think it develops as a result of our experiences. Many people feel that our sexual orientation is a result of a combination of both these factors.

Sexual orientation is sometimes thought of in terms of categories: heterosexual (when most or all of a person's attractions are directed toward people of the opposite sex); homosexual (when most or all of a person's attractions are directed toward people of his or her own sex); or bisexual (when someone has attractions toward people of both sexes).

Here are words you may have heard describing sexual orientation: "straight" (men who romantically love women, and women who romantically love men); "lesbian" (women who romantically love women); "gay" (men who romantically love men); and "bi" (men or women who romantically love both men and women). All are natural ways of being.

Many people reject the notion of putting people into categories and labeling them. Not everyone believes that people fit into one category or another.

In any event, the groupings don't apply to children, who are in the process of developing in all ways, including sexually.

Liking to hold hands, hug, and snuggle with friends of the same sex or of the opposite sex, or both, is common among kids. Sometimes sexual feelings

PFLAG (Parents, Family, and Friends of Lesbians and Gays) is a national organization that provides support for lesbian, gay, and bisexual people and their families. PFLAG's phone number is: (202) 638-4200.

accompany these affectionate gestures. These feelings don't necessarily predict what a person's sexual orientation will ultimately be.

✿ Sharing Romantic Feelings with a Partner

Slow dancing may be the first romantic physical contact a kid makes with another kid. When you are slow-dancing with someone, your heads may be close together. Your cheeks may be touching. Your heart may flutter a little.

Holding someone in your arms and dancing can be a way of expressing sexual feelings.

My First Kiss

The summer after fifth grade, I was invited to a boy-girl party. The hostess was an aggressive girl—bossy enough to have bullied her parents into staying out of the living room. As I remember, they sat in the kitchen, smoking Lucky Strike cigarettes and playing cards.

About twenty kids attended the party. When I arrived, the girls were standing against one wall whispering to one another, and the boys were monopolizing the chips and dip on the other side of the room.

"When I put on a record," the hostess announced, "everybody has to dance." She put a record on her portable green record player, and we listened to little thumps and scratchy noises, waiting for the music to begin. "Dance!" she told us. "I mean it!"

My boyfriend (meaning: the kid down the street who had given me a couple of rides on the handlebars of his bicycle) cautiously approached me. We held each other and began rocking back and forth to the music. I couldn't help but notice the dirt on his neck.

I tried to follow his lead gracefully, even though he seemed to be dancing to something entirely different from the music I was hearing.

"When I turn the lights out," barked the hostess, "kiss!" She flounced over and stood in the doorway with one finger on the light switch. I felt the tension mounting. The room went dark. "Kiss!" she shouted.

I quickly pulled my lips into my mouth and clamped my teeth on them. My boyfriend fumbled for my mouth but couldn't find my lips; they were safely tucked away. After bumping noses for a brief moment, he gave up and kissed my chin.

The next day, I broke up with this boy.

PEER PRESSURE ABOUT SEX

If you don't want to hug, kiss, slow-dance, or otherwise share romantic or sexual feelings with a partner, don't. You don't have to give a reason. You don't even need to have one.

Some Ways to Say **NO** to Peer Pressure

- "No. I don't care who's doing it; I'm not going to."

- "No. Don't try to pressure me into doing something that I don't feel right about."

- "You may feel it's okay, but I don't. And I don't like being pressured, so stop pressuring me."

No No No No

Don't let anyone talk you into sexual contact that you don't welcome. It's your body, and you have a right to say no, and your right to say no is protected by law. And—*don't pressure yourself*. Honor and respect your own ideas and instincts about what seems right for you.

Getting to Know Boys *Romantically*

Most parents set age limits on dating, and most preteens aren't allowed to date. But preteen kids who like each other romantically often talk on the phone and spend time together in groups, for example, at school activities, at church or temple or sports events, or at restaurants, the movies, or the mall.

It might seem hard to talk to a boy at first, but

when you're in a group, it's easier because there are other kids to interact with at the same time. But don't be surprised if a boy isn't all that responsive; boys generally begin to bloom socially a little later than girls.

Boys sometimes have an odd way of flirting; they might tease. They might toss broken cookies at you at a dance, instead of asking you to dance.

A little innocent teasing and playfulness is natural between boys and girls, of all ages! However, if it bothers you, say so. If it continues, tell the adult in charge.

SEXUAL HARASSMENT

Harassment is when someone bothers, disturbs, or torments another person.

Sexual harassment is when someone bothers another person with gestures, comments, jokes, wise-cracks, or questions that focus on sex, sexuality, gender, or certain physical characteristics—such as size of breasts, length of penis, or shape of legs.

Sexual harassment can also include *unwelcome* flirting or touching, as when one person makes continuous romantic overtures toward another person who isn't interested.

Remarks can be intended as compliments, like:

"Your legs look so long and sexy in high-heeled shoes!" Or they can be intended as insults, like: "Boy, you've got a big butt!" All unwelcome sexual comments are insults, whether they're intended to be positive or negative. And, either way, they can be considered sexual harassment.

Sexual harassment is harmful for a lot of reasons. One is that it can interfere with the development of natural, confident feelings about one's sexual self.

If a kid (or kids) sexually harasses you at school or on the bus or anywhere else, tell the person to stop. If the harassment continues, report it to your parents and ask them to talk to your teacher, principal, or the adult in charge.

If you feel sexually harassed by an adult, *always* report it to your parent or another adult in charge. It's extremely inappropriate for an adult to make sexual comments to a child, and it's criminal for an adult to have sexual contact with a child—in all cases. And in all cases—it's *never* considered the kid's fault (see pages 160–168).

General Harassment

Harassment isn't limited to sexual harassment. Unfortunately, there are kids who enjoy making others miserable by saying and doing mean-spirited things. If this is happening to you at school, know that the problem lies with them, not with you—but it *becomes* your problem if you don't ask for help dealing with a situation. At school, you have a right to be free of harassment. It is part of every teacher's job to supervise student behavior, including social behavior. Ask your teacher, counselor, or principal when it would be a good time to discuss a problem you may be having with another student and to help come up with a plan of action. If you feel it would be helpful, have your parent attend the meeting with you.

Chapter 9

MORE ABOUT
SEX

❀ Love and Sex

Love is a profoundly tender, passionate affection for another person. For most adults, sex is a reflection of loving feelings—an intimate way of communicating love. But not all adult couples have sex. Loving couples can find many ways to express love without having sex.

Some adults enjoy sexual relationships with consenting friends or acquaintances—without being in love. But for most people, sex and love are linked.

Many people consider sex to be a sacred act, an intimate expression of love—which should be reserved for partners who are married to each other.

Others think of it this way: Sex is an intimate expression of love, reserved for partners who are committed to a long-term, mutually faithful relationship based on love and trust.

There are lots of good reasons to postpone having

sex with a partner. One of the best reasons is that it's worth the wait, if we wait until we are grown and in love with someone who loves us in return. When linked with love, sex can be one of the most powerful, intense, and satisfying experiences two people can share.

✿ Kids and Love

Sometimes kids fall in love with each other. But kids are not yet equipped to cope with the complex set of emotions that accompany a sexual relationship. And kids are not able to fully accept the responsibility that goes along with having sex with a partner (see pages 99–100).

> It's important to become familiar with the following information *well in advance* of becoming sexually active with a partner. Knowing the facts about sex can help you make informed decisions in the future.

✿ CONSENT

Sharing sexual feelings with a partner requires consent. Consent may be withheld or withdrawn by either partner at any time. This is true for all couples, including married couples. When one person says no, the other person has to stop. That's the rule, and that's the law.

Our laws protect all people of all ages from being forced (either by physical force or verbal threat) into sexual contact. This is true even if they have freely agreed to have sexual contact in the past.

Please note that *consented-to* sexual contact between young couples is only considered to be *consented-to* if the kids are of similar ages. No matter what anyone agrees to, it is never okay for sexual contact to occur between two kids who are not in a similar age group (see page 162).

PEER PRESSURE ABOUT CONSENT

As You Grow Up, Stay in Charge:

Most boys are respectful and considerate regarding the issue of consent. But on occasion, a girl may encounter a boy who says things to try to convince her to consent to sexual contact when she doesn't want to. For example, he may say that he'll be in physical pain if he doesn't get to have an orgasm after he's become sexually aroused (turned on).

A boy who's sexually aroused might experience a little discomfort and disappointment when he's told no by a girl, but he'll get over it. In any event, this should have no influence on a girl's decision to say no.

It can be very harmful for someone to say yes when she doesn't want to say yes. It can never hurt someone to be told no to sex. And even if it could, a girl's responsibility is to *herself*.

Another approach a boy might use to try to convince a girl to give consent is to say, "If you cared about me as much as I care about you, you'd agree to do this with me." Or, "If you love me, prove it."

Caring about someone means truly respecting their feelings. It does *not* include pressuring someone to do something they don't feel right about. We do not have to prove affection by consenting to sexual contact, and we should not be asked to do so.

THE BIG ALERT

It's possible that a boy might become aggressive when a girl decides to end sexual contact. He may say something like: "You started this, and now you have to finish it!"

A girl should be very concerned if she hears a statement like this. It's calculated to make her feel guilty, responsible, or even threatened. These kinds of words are signals for her to protect herself by immediately ending contact with this boy. She may also need to discuss what happened with a trusted adult (see pages 160–164).

Since people are unique beings, we like different things—different foods, different clothes, different music and movies. We also have different preferences regarding physical touching. Religious and cultural traditions, as well as health considerations and sexual orientation, play significant roles in the decisions people make about what kind of touching they believe should be included in a sexual relationship with a partner. As you read the material that follows, keep in mind that sexual contact—no matter what kind—always requires permission from the people involved.

❀ Definitions:

Making Out

"Making out" is when two people hug and kiss in a prolonged, romantic way. Sometimes they "French-kiss." This is open-mouthed kissing, including tongues.

GOING FURTHER

"Going further" refers to other ways that people can touch each other sexually while making out. This can include touching the breasts, clitoris, or vagina of a partner; it can include touching the penis and testicles of a partner. Going further can include caressing any part of the body, with or without clothing.

Making out and going further can arouse strong sexual responses. Often, one or both people have orgasms while making out and touching each other's private places (see page 91).

Sexual Intercourse

Sexual intercourse is a major landmark in a romantic relationship and is described on pages 99-101.

Oral Sex

A friend overheard her young daughter and her daughter's friends giggling about oral sex. Later, the mother asked her daughter, "Do you know what oral sex is?"

"Mom!" said her daughter. "Everybody knows what oral sex is."

"Then what is it?" said her mother.

"It's talking dirty on the phone."

Pretty good guess, but not quite right. *Oral* refers to the mouth. *Oral sex* refers to sexual activity that includes stimulating one's partner's genitals by using the lips, mouth, and tongue.

Anal Sex

Stimulating the area in or around the anus is sometimes included in sexual activity between some partners.

Anal sex generally refers to partners having sexual intercourse by way of the anus.

STD

A sexually transmitted disease (STD) is a disease that can be passed from one person to another during sexual contact.

Sexual intercourse, oral sex, and especially anal sex put people at risk for becoming exposed to the germs that can cause sexually transmitted diseases, including AIDS (see pages 124–143).

Acting Responsibly

Aside from moral or religious considerations of family traditions and values, there may be health consequences to having sex with a partner. These may include getting sexually transmitted diseases and getting pregnant.

Engaging in sex with a partner brings with it the responsibility of *knowing how* to reduce the risks of transmitting sexually transmitted diseases and acting to reduce the risk in all ways possible. It includes being willing and able to seek medical care if there is suspected exposure to a sexually transmitted disease. (For more on STDs, see pages 131–143.)

Acting responsibly also includes *knowing how* to take precautions to avoid unplanned pregnancy, and *acting* to prevent unplanned pregnancy.

In the United States, a teenage boy or girl gets a sexually transmitted disease every fifteen seconds.

In the United States, a teenage girl gets pregnant every thirty seconds.

These statistics tell us something: Most teenagers who *feel* ready to have sex with a partner aren't *actually* ready.

✿ YOURS TO DISCOVER AND EXPLORE

As you grow and change, remember that your sexuality is an amazing and wondrous part of you. It is yours to discover and explore, and it will be yours to share with a partner when you are grown up. Sex is a natural, important part of life.

When you are fully mature—aware of and ready and able to accept the risks and responsibilities involved in having sex with a partner and willing and able to make the commitment required—you will be in a position to say yes to someone you love and trust, and will feel comfortable and happy in a sexual relationship that is right for both of you.

Chapter 10

CONDOMS

❀ Discovering Condoms

A friend told me that when she was a kid, she happened to be snooping in her father's top drawer, hoping to find a mint. Instead, she found a weird-looking, rolled-up clear balloon!

She unrolled it and blew it up as big as she could get it. It was one of the best balloons she had ever seen, and one of the easiest to blow up, since the opening was so wide!

Yippee!

She was batting it around the room like a maniac when her big brother walked in. "Look!" she cried. "Isn't this a great balloon!"

"Mom?" he called. "I think you'd better come up and see the balloon Linda found...."

Her mother hurried up the stairs and into the room and said something like: "Yes! Isn't that a nice balloon," whacking it away from her and catching it. "But it's Dad's balloon, Linda, not yours. And Dad likes to keep his balloons for himself, so leave it alone.

And quit jumping on my bed. And straighten up the bedspread! Look what a mess you made!"

My friend said she remembered thinking it was stingy of her father, whom she had never even seen play with a balloon, to have a secret stash of balloons that he wasn't willing to share with the rest of the family.

But it wasn't a balloon. It was a condom!

✿ CONDOMS

A *condom* is a covering for the penis that a male can wear during sex. It's made of very thin, delicate material—usually latex (a kind of rubber). Condoms are used for two purposes: to help prevent the spread of sexually transmitted diseases (STDs) and to prevent unplanned pregnancy.

Not all condoms are made of latex. Some are made of natural membrane (lambskin). Certain germs can pass through condoms made of natural membrane. These germs cannot pass through latex. That is why a condom worn to prevent the spread of sexually transmitted diseases must be made of latex.

HELPING PREVENT THE SPREAD OF STDs

A condom provides a thin barrier between a male's penis and the body of his partner. It prevents skin-to-skin contact. Germs for certain sexually transmitted diseases (STDs) can be found in the semen, preseminal fluid, vaginal fluid, cervical secretions, or blood—including menstrual blood—of someone who is infected. Some germs can also be present in sores or on the skin.

When used correctly, latex condoms help protect both partners from the spread of germs that might enter the body through the mucous membrane at the tip of the penis, or the mucous membranes inside the vagina, through cuts or scratches or sores, or by other contact with the skin.

If the condom is put on as soon as the penis is erect, a male's preseminal fluid will be prevented from coming in contact with his partner's body. If ejaculation occurs, the condom will trap the semen.

✿ HELPING PREVENT UNPLANNED PREGNANCY

Since a condom prevents preseminal fluid and semen, both of which contain sperm, from landing near or inside a female's vagina, a condom, used correctly, will prevent pregnancy—especially if used with *spermicide*, which kills sperm (see page 147).

Condoms Are *Not* 100 Percent Effective

Condoms aren't 100 percent effective. They can break and they can fall off. But, when used correctly *every single time*, they offer a great deal of protection against the spread of disease and against unplanned pregnancy.

Using a Lubricant

A latex condom needs to be lubricated (made slippery) in order to make sure it won't tear during intercourse. The lubricant must be water-based because oil-based lubricants (such as Vaseline or butter) can damage condoms.

Water-based lubricants usually come in a tube, and are sold in drugstores.

The lubricant is put on the outside of the condom *after* the condom has been rolled onto the penis. Water-based lubricant should be used in addition to the lubricant that already may be on a latex condom.

Some water-based lubricants contain spermicide (see page 147).

For Your Information...

Even though it's the male who wears a condom, using a condom correctly is the shared responsibility of both partners.

Basic condom tips include these:

◆ **A condom should be made of *latex*.** It should *not* be made of natural membrane (lambskin).

◆ A condom should be inspected in good light. A condom that has already been unrolled, is brittle or torn, or feels sticky or is stuck to itself should be thrown out.

◆ If the expiration date on the package has passed, the condoms shouldn't be used.

◆ Condoms come rolled up in individual packets and, because condoms are delicate, the packets must be opened carefully.

◆ The rolled-up ring of the condom should be facing the outside.

◆ A half-inch space must be left at the tip, and this space must be gently pinched closed before and during the unrolling of the condom onto the penis. This is true even if there is a "reservoir tip." The condom should be unrolled all the way to the pubic hair, covering the entire penis.

◆ If the condom doesn't roll on correctly the first time, the partners must start again *with a new condom*.

◆ After sex, while the penis is still erect, the male should pull his penis out of his partner's body slowly, **holding the condom in place with his hand** to avoid spilling semen. He should turn and move completely away from his partner before letting go of the condom.

◆ A *new condom* must be used each time.

◆ Condoms should be stored in a cool place.

Shopping for Condoms

Condoms are sold in drugstores and also in some grocery stores and convenience stores. They are usually located in the same section that has deodorant, pads, and other personal products—or near the register.

Anyone can buy condoms. They are relatively inexpensive; the price depends on how many are in the box. (Some clinics give out free condoms. The county health department usually knows where one can get free condoms.)

A box of condoms often has a romantic picture on the front, such as a man and a woman looking deep into each other's eyes with the moon rising behind them. The brand name is usually in large print on the box. Inside the box, condoms come rolled up and individually wrapped in foil or plastic packets.

There are many different kinds of condoms. Some are lubricated. Some are not. Some say "textured." Some have reservoir tips; some don't.

An inexperienced condom shopper mostly needs to look for three things:

• The word *latex* should be on the box.

• A "disease prevention claim" should be printed someplace on the box. The claim will say something like: "These latex condoms, when properly used, may help reduce the risk of catching or spreading many sexually transmitted diseases."

• There should be an expiration date on the box, and it should not have passed.

> At the time of publication of this book, *latex* condoms are considered the safest condom choice. However, other materials for making condoms are being investigated and tested. Stay informed! Talk to your pharmacist or health care professional about any new developments.

✿ A Reminder

Males sometimes resist wearing condoms. Some say condoms decrease their sexual pleasure. Some may promise to "pull out" before ejaculating. However, since preseminal fluid can contain sperm and/or the germs that cause STDs, "pulling out" doesn't work! Another thing that doesn't work about "pulling out" is that guys often goof up and don't pull out in time. The male may ejaculate inside the female, and she may become pregnant (and/or get an STD) as a result.

Chapter 11

A sexually transmitted disease (STD) is a disease that can be spread from one person to another through sexual contact. How the disease is spread depends upon the STD.

Sexually transmitted diseases include: warts on the vagina, cervix, or penis, chlamydia, herpes simplex, gonorrhea, syphilis, hepatitis B, HIV, and many others. These diseases are all caused by germs—either bacteria or viruses. Even cancer of the cervix is now known to be caused by a virus that is spread by sexual intercourse.

STDs are spread in a variety of ways, depending on the STD

Preseminal fluid and semen sometimes contain the germs that cause certain sexually transmitted diseases. Vaginal fluid, cervical secretions, and menstrual blood may also contain these germs. In some cases, germs may be present in sores on the skin.

> **The chances of transmission of certain STDs can be reduced by wearing a condom (see pages 125–126).**

Treating Sexually Transmitted Diseases

Some sexually transmitted diseases are completely curable—provided they are treated in time. Chlamydia, gonorrhea, and syphilis are examples of STDs that can be cured with antibiotics. If not treated in time, though, these infections can cause permanent damage (for example, the inability to become pregnant). Syphilis, if left untreated, may eventually lead to death.

Gonorrhea and chlamydia often have no *symptoms* (outward signs of infection) in women, or have very mild symptoms—which go unnoticed. Some women suffer permanent damage to their reproductive organs before they realize they're infected.

Chlamydia is especially troublesome, since it's very common and since most young men who have it don't know they have it—so they don't get treated, and, of course, don't warn their partners.

But people can be tested for STDs, even if there are no symptoms. STDs are one reason why sexually active people need to schedule routine checkups.

Other sexually transmitted diseases, such as herpes simplex and warts, cannot be cured but are manageable. An infected person learns to manage the symptoms with medical advice and medication.

Crabs

Crabs are little creatures similar to head lice. They live in pubic hair. Crabs cause a person infected with them to itch. They are usually spread by sexual contact, but sometimes are passed along on towels, bedding, or clothing. Crabs can be eliminated by an over-the-counter product sold at the drugstore. Ask the pharmacist.

AIDS

AIDS (acquired immunodeficiency syndrome) is a disease that can be transmitted sexually. It is caused by a virus called HIV (human immunodeficiency virus). The virus lives in the blood (including menstrual blood), semen, preseminal fluid, and vaginal fluid and cervical secretions of an infected person. It can also be present in the milk of a nursing mother who is infected with HIV.

The HIV virus can be passed from one person to another if any of these fluids from an infected person enters someone else's body. The virus can enter through a break in the skin or through the mucous membranes of the mouth, tip of penis, vagina, or anus (or nose or eyes). The virus can be passed from an infected pregnant woman to her unborn child and it can be passed through breast-feeding.

Most HIV infections occur when people have sex without effectively using a latex condom, or when people share the needles and syringes used to inject illegal drugs, including steroids.

Anyone—young or old, rich or poor, gay, straight, or bisexual—exposed to the HIV virus can become infected. People who are infected are said to be "HIV positive." *You can't tell by looking at someone if he or she*

Even though there isn't a cure for AIDS, we can prevent HIV from spreading. If you don't have sex with a partner or share drug equipment, and if you avoid other people's blood, you won't be at risk for becoming infected with HIV and developing AIDS.

has been infected by HIV. There are no outward clues until a person gets sick—which may be years after the virus has entered that person's body. A person infected with HIV may not know it, and can infect others without meaning to.

HIV attacks the immune system, which is the body's system for fighting off infections. Over time, as the body loses the ability to recover from sicknesses, the infected person reaches a point at which he or she is said to have AIDS. There is a lot we don't know about HIV and AIDS; we do know that the disease has killed millions of people worldwide. As of yet, there is no cure for AIDS—although medications that prolong life for some people with AIDS are now available.

"Don't Wait for Me"

A friend of mine enjoyed going to the movies with her older brother, a teacher. One evening, on their way to the theater, they entered the crosswalk of a busy intersection. "Run!" her brother said, when he saw that the light had changed. "Don't wait for me!"

My friend hurried across to the other side and watched, terrified, as her brother slowly crossed. A car honked and skidded to a stop.

"I forgot to tell you," he said when he reached the other side. "I can't run anymore."

Over the months that followed, this brother and sister continued going to the movies together. After the movie ended, my friend waited patiently until her brother was able to stand up long enough to gain his balance and walk out of the theater. It took him several tries.

"He just wanted to be able to stand up by himself," she later told me.

Weeks later, my friend sat with her brother as he was dying of AIDS. Somebody realized that his request for cremation hadn't been signed, but he was too weak to sign it. "They say it's okay if you just make an X," his sister told him. "Can you make an X if I hold the paper?"

My friend's brother sat up. With great concentration, he wrote his whole name on the paper while his sister held it.

A few days later, he died.

Sisters all over the United States and all over the world are losing their brothers to AIDS—and brothers are losing their sisters. Parents are losing their sons and daughters; aunts and uncles are losing their nieces and nephews; grandparents are losing their grandchildren. Friends and lovers are losing each other. Children are losing their family members, too.

It can be sad and scary to think about AIDS. But

remember that knowing how HIV is spread can help us protect ourselves and one another.

HIV and Blood

Skin acts like a protective barrier, but skin can't protect us from HIV if the skin is broken. If skin is scraped, cut, or scratched, or if there is a rash, the virus can easily pass through. Remember that HIV can pass into mucous membranes (even if there is no break in the membrane).

Avoid coming into direct contact with other people's blood, including bloody noses, cuts, sores, scratches, bloody bandages, and menstrual fluid.

Ear-piercing "guns" and body-piercing equipment are not always sterile and must be to prevent transmitting the HIV virus. If you have your ears or body pierced in a store or salon, have your parents make sure that the equipment is properly sterilized. It's safest to have piercing done by a health care professional.

Be aware that there are guidelines for manicurists (people who "do" nails). Tools should be sterilized or disposable so that only clean tools come in contact with your nails and skin.

Unsterile tattoo equipment can spread HIV.

To stay on the safe side, don't share toothbrushes,

razors, or earrings for pierced ears, which may have some fresh blood on them.

If You Know Someone with HIV or AIDS

Many children are born infected with HIV, since an infected pregnant woman can pass it to her unborn child.

If you know someone with HIV or AIDS, you *can't* get it by sitting near, talking to, hugging, or holding hands with the person. If you want to show affection in this way, do. People with HIV or AIDS need support, compassion, understanding, and acceptance—just like everybody else.

Keep hope alive. Research that is going on all over the world is leading to ways to better manage the disease until a cure is found.

MAKiNG OUT and STDs

Under certain conditions, making out can pose a risk of exposure to sexually transmitted diseases.

Although hepatitis B is usually spread through sexual intercourse, the virus which causes it may be present in saliva. Therefore, it's possible for hepatitis B to be spread by kissing. Whether or not you plan to kiss, talk to your doctor about becoming immunized against hepatitis B.

Herpes is in a special category. A cold sore on the mouth (oral herpes) isn't considered an STD. But oral herpes can be spread through kissing. The herpes virus present in a cold sore can be passed to the genitals of a partner during oral sex. Once spread to the genitals, the partner will have genital herpes. A herpes sore on the genitals (genital herpes) can be spread to a partner's mouth during oral sex, whereupon the partner will have oral herpes. Genital herpes can be spread during genital-to-genital contact.

Small amounts of the HIV virus have been found in saliva, but at the time of publication of this book, there have been no documented instances of HIV having been spread by kissing alone.

However, it must be pointed out that HIV could be spread through kissing if blood is present in the mouth of an infected person and saliva is exchanged. (HIV present in the blood could be absorbed by the mucous membranes of the mouth.)

People who have cuts, scratches, or other breaks in the skin—including the skin on the hands— should not have sexual contact that would allow pre-seminal fluid, semen, blood, or vaginal fluid to get into these breaks.

Information about sexual contact and sexually transmitted diseases can be confusing—and can change. If you have specific questions about exposure to sexually transmitted diseases through kissing, making out, "going further," or other contact, you can call the CDC National STD Hotline and they will answer your questions or refer you to someone in your area who can:

1-800-227-8922 (U.S. only)
1-800-243-7889 (TTY)

The call is free, confidential, and won't appear on the phone bill.

Information about tests for sexually transmitted diseases is available through the local health department, at family planning clinics such as Planned Parenthood, or at a doctor's office (or by calling the CDC National STD Hotline–U.S. only).

Sexual Intercourse and STDs

Sexual intercourse is high-risk activity for spreading sexually transmitted diseases since STD germs may be present in preseminal fluid, semen, vaginal fluids, menstrual blood, cervical secretions, and in sores on the genitals (see pages 138–139).

Oral Sex and STDs

Oral sex is risky activity for spreading sexually transmitted diseases. Germs that cause certain sexually transmitted diseases may be present in the mouth as well as in the genitals.

Since HIV may be present in preseminal fluid, semen, vaginal fluid, blood, and menstrual blood; and since HIV can be absorbed through mucous membranes, which line the mouth, oral sex is considered risky sexual contact. Withdrawing the penis before ejaculation doesn't completely remove the risk, since preseminal fluid can contain the HIV virus (see page 139).

An unlubricated latex condom worn by the male during oral sex can provide a protective barrier between his penis and his partner's mouth.

Household plastic wrap (or a latex condom cut in half lengthwise, or a dental dam) can provide a protective barrier to separate the mouth from the vaginal area during oral sex performed on a female, although the effectiveness of this method has not been proved.

Anal Sex and STDs

Because the anus and rectal area are easily torn or bruised, and because of the presence of mucous membranes, anal sex is very high-risk sexual activity for becoming infected with HIV and other STDs.

Also, bacteria that are present in the rectum can cause health problems when spread elsewhere.

> A condom can easily break during anal sex. *Water-based* lubricant spread on the outside of a latex condom (after the condom is on the penis) makes breaking less likely (see page 127).

HIV and Drugs

Since blood from one person can be left in a hypodermic needle and syringe, sharing needles or other drug equipment is a common way for HIV (and other diseases) to be passed from one person to another. And once infected, people can go on to infect their sexual partners as well as those people with whom they may be sharing needles and syringes (see page 137).

People Who Are Sexually Active May Reduce the Risk of Becoming Exposed to HIV if:

The male wears a latex condom that's lubricated with *water-based* lubricant during every single act of sexual intercourse or anal sex.

There is a barrier between partners' mouths and genitals during every single act of oral sex (see page 141).

Partners stay informed regarding new developments and information regarding HIV and new kinds of protective products and strategies.

remember:

Other methods of birth control—such as birth control pills or foam—*do not protect* either partner from becoming exposed to HIV.

If you have questions about HIV, HIV testing, or HIV/AIDS counseling, call the CDC National HIV/AIDS Hotline and ask.

It's free (U.S. only).

The number is:
1-800-342-AIDS (2437)
1-800-243-7889 (TTY)
1-800-344-7432
(Spanish language)

The call will not appear on the phone bill.

In Canada, you may consult your local health department, listed in the municipality section of the white pages in the phonebook, or call the information operator (411) for an HIV/AIDS information hotline.

Chapter 12

Birth Control

and Unplanned Pregnancy

❀

A TRIP TO THE MARKET

When my friend Mark was in junior high, his mother sent him to the corner market to buy some coffee. The coffee beans could be ground in a machine installed in the store aisle.

Mark chose a bag of beans and poured them into the machine. He put the empty bag under a metal spout at the bottom. Then he pushed the "on" button.

Meanwhile, Lucy, a girl he knew, had come into the market. It was a very small market, with narrow aisles. Mark bent over to get a closer look at the machine; at the same moment, on the opposite side of the aisle, Lucy also bent over to pick out a can from the bottom shelf.

They accidentally bumped rumps!

Mark and Lucy both stood up quickly. Mark apologized, but Lucy hurried out of the store. She went

home and, sobbing, told her mother that a boy named Mark had made her pregnant in the market.

After a frantic phone call to Mark's mother and further clarification from Lucy, it was established that there had been a misunderstanding: Lucy had heard that people get pregnant by "bumping and grinding." This is an old-time expression for having sex.

There are lots of different expressions for having sex—too many to list. But there's only one way a girl or a woman can get pregnant: semen or preseminal fluid from a male must get close to the opening of, or inside, her vagina.

Birth Control

To avoid conceiving children while having sexual intercourse, most people practice birth control. Birth control may take the form of condoms or other "barriers," chemicals, hormonal contraceptives, or surgical sterilization. No birth control method is 100 percent effective.

Some people reject the use of these methods, and instead stress "timing intercourse" as a means of family planning. This involves trying to avoid pregnancy by making an educated guess about when ovulation might occur and avoiding sex at that time. Timing intercourse, sometimes known as using the *rhythm method*, is not an effective method of birth control.

Some couples attempt to prevent pregnancy by withdrawal of the penis before ejaculation. This doesn't work. Preseminal fluid contains sperm; also, it's easy for the male to fail to withdraw in time.

METHODS OF BIRTH CONTROL

Before a couple begins having sexual intercourse, a visit to a family planning clinic, the health department, a doctor's office, and/or a drugstore is in order.

Barriers and Chemicals

Barrier methods of birth control prevent sperm from coming in contact with an egg.

A condom, as you know, fits over the man's penis, trapping the sperm when he ejaculates. The *diaphragm* and *cervical cap* are other barrier methods of birth control. These are worn by the woman. Diaphragms and cervical caps must be prescribed by a health care practitioner. They are small latex cups inserted into the vagina before intercourse. They fit snugly over the cervix. Both are used with spermicide, which kills sperm on contact.

Spermicides come in many different forms, including gels, foams, and suppositories. Spermicides must be used in combination with a condom, diaphragm, or cervical cap to be effective for birth control.

Diaphragms and cervical caps do *not* provide protection from sexually transmitted diseases.

Hormonal Contraceptives

Hormonal contraceptives cause changes in the way a woman's reproductive system is regulated by hormones and prevent pregnancy. They must be prescribed by a doctor. Hormonal contraceptives include oral pills ("the Pill"), implants, and injections. These are effective for birth control, but do not provide protection from sexually transmitted diseases.

The Pill is a highly effective and relatively safe way of preventing pregnancy. Some people are prescribed the Pill to regulate their hormones or their periods.

Taken daily, it contains two hormones, both of which normally fluctuate with a woman's monthly cycle. The hormones stop an egg from being released by the ovary. They also change the secretions of the cervix so that sperm cannot get through. Most women feel fine while on the Pill, but some have side effects; side effects should be discussed with the doctor.

People relying on the Pill for birth control must take it *exactly* as instructed to avoid becoming pregnant. (Missing even *one* Pill could result in pregnancy.)

Many factors can interfere with the Pill's effectiveness, including bouts of vomiting or diarrhea, as well as certain medications (including some kinds of antibiotics). It's very important to read and follow the instructions inside the packaging for the Pill.

Contraceptive implants contain a hormone found in the Pill. They also prevent ovulation and keep the sperm from getting through the cervix. Implants are inserted by a health care professional in the upper arm, and they last for several years.

The *injectable contraceptive* uses a shorter-acting hormone. It is effective for three months per injection. Many women experience side effects from injections and implants. But others find them to be a satisfactory alternative to having to remember to take the Pill at the same time every day.

Intrauterine Device (IUD)

An intrauterine device (IUD) is a small device a doctor puts into the uterus to prevent pregnancy. It is not recommended for young people because of the high risk of infection associated with its use.

Surgical Sterilization

Sterilization surgery is a more permanent means of birth control. It involves cutting and closing a woman's Fallopian tubes (this surgery is also called *tubal ligation* or "having one's tubes tied"), or cutting and removing part of the duct that transports sperm to a man's penis (called a *vasectomy*). Surgery for birth control isn't used unless a person feels absolutely certain that he or she does not wish to have children—or more children—ever. It's not considered appropriate for young people.

A Reminder

Latex condoms are the only form of birth control that can significantly help protect people against sexually transmitted diseases, including HIV. Sexually active people must *always* use a latex condom to help prevent the spread of disease, regardless of what other birth control method is being used.

BIRTH CONTROL

A WORD ABOUT SAFETY AND SIDE EFFECTS

The *safest* method of birth control is to not have sex (*abstinence*). Loving couples can find many ways to express love without having sex. But for those couples who do decide to have sex, it's important to remember that sexually transmitted diseases and pregnancy pose more of a health threat than birth control. The topic of birth control should be discussed with parents, a trusted older relative or friend, a counselor, the school nurse, a doctor, or a health care professional in a family planning clinic before making a decision about having sex.

Birth Control for Youth

Anyone can buy latex condoms and water-based lubricant at a drugstore.

Spermicidal foams, gels, creams, and contraceptive suppositories offer increased protection in case a condom breaks, leaks, or slips off; these also can be bought at the drugstore without a prescription. Spermicidal foams, gels, creams, and contraceptive suppositories are *not* effective when used alone.

In addition, birth control—including prescribed birth control—is available for kids as young as thirteen—without their parents' knowledge or consent. (Minors are considered to have a right to privacy in certain matters regarding their health.)

The combination of a latex condom worn by the male and lubricated on the outside with a water-based lubricant to help prevent it from breaking *plus* a spermicidal foam, gel, or suppository used by the female both helps prevent pregnancy and substantially reduces the risk of being infected with a sexually transmitted disease. Anyone—including kids—can buy these products without a prescription.

Planned Parenthood and local departments of public health are examples of places that will provide birth control for kids. Free birth control may be available for kids who can't afford it.

Emergency Hormonal Contraception

Doctors, hospital emergency departments, and family planning clinics may be able to provide emergency hormonal contraception for a girl or woman who has had unprotected intercourse (i.e., did not use birth control or used birth control that failed). The medication is effective only if taken within a certain time frame, and must be given under appropriate medical supervision. (A health care professional should be notified *as soon as possible* after the unprotected intercourse, even if it means calling on the weekend.) The medication works by either keeping the ovary from releasing an egg or changing the lining of the uterus so

> There is a toll-free number that anyone can call to find out the location of the nearest office of Planned Parenthood: 1-800-230-7526 (U.S. only)
> In Canada, consult your local directory or call 411 to find the Planned Parenthood office nearest you.

that a fertilized egg may not attach and develop. Emergency hormonal contraception is not 100 percent effective and is *not* a routine method of birth control.

Pregnancy Tests

Usually, the first sign of pregnancy is a missed period. Some women, though, experience very light periods (or spotting) during pregnancy.

Pregnancy tests can be conducted in a clinic, in a doctor's office, or at home. Home pregnancy tests are easy to use and available at drugstores and supermarkets.

BELIEVE IT!

A girl *can* get pregnant the first time she has sexual intercourse—and many girls do. A girl *can* get pregnant if the couple stands up while having sexual intercourse. A girl *can* get pregnant when she is having her period. A girl *can* get pregnant before she begins to menstruate—because she may be ovulating for the very first time!

Some home pregnancy tests can be used as early as one day after the period is due. But the waiting time on tests varies; information and instructions are in the packaging.

> A person who is pregnant or who suspects she is pregnant should make an appointment with a doctor right away. She should not drink alcohol, smoke cigarettes, or take drugs. Prescribed medicines may need to be changed. She should not have an X ray unless her doctor ordering the X ray and the person operating the X-ray machine know she's pregnant. A person who is pregnant or suspects she is pregnant should not change the cat litter box, dig in the dirt without gloves, eat raw or rare fish or meat, or eat undercooked eggs. These things could cause health problems for the baby growing inside her.

✿ Choices for the Pregnant Teen

When a girl becomes pregnant without planning to, she has to make choices. In most cases, telling parents right away is the first, best choice a girl can make. Even though it is difficult to tell, parents can lend support and get information to help a pregnant teen make decisions about her unplanned pregnancy.

Counseling is available in every community. The

doctor's office is a good place to start. Planned Parenthood can provide directions to the nearest clinic (1-800-230-7526). The *county health department* can also provide counseling information (call 411, or look under "county government" listings in the phone book). Counseling is confidential. It is available regardless of whether the pregnant girl has told her parents or not. In order to have all the options available, a pregnant teen must get counseling as soon as she realizes she is pregnant.

Her options include the following:

- Give birth to the baby and raise it—perhaps with the help of family, or government programs set up to help teen parents.
- Give birth to the baby and arrange for a *legal* adoption through a state or county government agency, a licensed private agency, or a licensed attorney.
- Give birth to the baby and, with the help of a government agency, have the baby placed in foster care until the teen mom is in a position to raise the baby herself.
- Have a legal abortion performed by a health care professional—provided the pregnancy is in its early stages. An abortion is a proce-

dure that ends a pregnancy. In some, but not all, states, parents' consent is required for abortions for women under eighteen. The option of abortion is *not* available if a girl waits too long to schedule one. Pregnancy counselors can help a girl arrange payment for the abortion.

The father of the baby has both rights and responsibilities. While he cannot interfere with the girl's right to an early abortion, he can have some say in allowing the baby to be adopted or placed in foster care. He also can be held legally responsible for financial support until his child is an adult.

Chapter 13

STAYING SAFE

It Happened to Me

One summer when I was a kid, I was invited along on a friend's family vacation. We stayed in a house on the beach for two weeks—and it was the first time I had been away from home alone.

There were lifeguard stations along the beach, where cute guys (much older than we were) sat in tall chairs, looking out at the surf. My friend and I liked flirting with the lifeguards, by walking past in our bikinis and waving and giggling.

One evening, my friend and I were allowed to go to a carnival by ourselves, about five miles away. We felt pretty mature, being permitted to go alone. When her mom dropped us off, she told us to be sure to get the nine o'clock bus home.

After we were at the carnival for an hour or so, a lifeguard we recognized came over and started talking to my friend—who was then eleven years old. "We'll be right back," she told me. "Just wait here."

My friend and the lifeguard didn't come right back. I waited, pretending to have fun watching the people on the rides. Finally, they reappeared—holding hands.

"He's taking us home," my friend told me. She gave me a sly look.

"We're supposed to take the bus," I said.

"You missed the last bus," the lifeguard said. "Don't worry—I'll drive you."

"Well, what do you want to do?" my friend asked me. "Walk five miles home in the dark? I'm going with him, whether you come or not."

I didn't feel quite right about the arrangement, but I thought, Oh, well. After all, he *is* a lifeguard...

I followed them to his car. He opened the back door for me, and I saw that a young man was sitting in the backseat. At this point, I felt that going in the car was a bad idea. But I was worried about my friend going off alone with these two guys. So I got in.

On the way back to the beach house, my friend sat very close to the lifeguard in the front. Just after we pulled out onto the highway, the man sitting in the back with me began touching my breasts and forcing his hand between my legs. I tried to fight him off, but

158

he overpowered me. I kept crying out and trying to push him away.

As we drove into town, the light turned red. The car stopped. I shouted to my friend, "Get out of the car! Get out of the car!" I pulled free of the man. Both my friend and I scrambled out onto the sidewalk and ran home.

"Whatever you do, don't tell my mom," my friend told me before we went into the house.

This was *very* bad advice.

I didn't tell her mom or anyone else. I felt scared of the man who assaulted me—and the lifeguard. I felt alone and missed my family. I blamed myself; I thought people would blame me if they knew what had happened. I felt sick whenever I thought of what had happened in the car. I tried to forget, but the bad feelings lingered on. The experience stayed with me for years, like a shadow in the back of my mind.

It makes me sad to think of myself all alone with those scary feelings and memories. I should have called my mom right away; I needed help. Since my mom didn't know what happened, she couldn't comfort me. She couldn't help me realize I wasn't to blame.

I wish I could go back through time and put my arms around myself when I was a girl and say, "I'm sorry such a rotten thing happened to such a great kid."

FORCED CONTACT

Forced or unconsented-to sexual touching is wrong and illegal no matter what. It is commonly called "sexual assault." Actually, any unconsented-to sexual contact is "sexual battery." Regardless of the term used, sexual contact that occurs without both partners' permission is against the law.

Rape is forced sexual intercourse.

Acquaintance rape (or "date rape") is rape that can happen in the context of people getting to know each other romantically. Basically, what happens is that one person fails to honor the word *no*, and forces the other

Rape Crisis Hotline numbers are available in almost all communities. The information operator (411) can provide a Rape Crisis Hotline number. It is also important to call the police, the emergency room of the hospital, or the Child Help IOF Forester's National Child Abuse Hotline:

1-800-4-A-CHILD
1-800-2-A-CHILD (TTY)

into having sexual intercourse—often after they have been kissing, making out, or touching each other sexually.

Acquaintance rape is just as illegal and wrong as rape; both are serious criminal offenses—felonies, punishable by jail. Anyone who is raped should get medical attention immediately (see pages 152–153).

If someone—anyone, including another kid—forces or scares you into any form of sexual contact, remember: It's not your fault. Don't blame yourself. Tell your parent, doctor, or teacher, or a police officer, or another adult you trust—right away.

Sexual Abuse of Kids

Some sexual abuse of kids is forced. Some sexual abuse of kids involves scaring or threatening kids into sexual contact. But often a sexual abuser will try to trick, confuse, or seduce a kid into having sexual contact. The abuser will try to take advantage of the fact that the kid has less experience than the abuser.

A sexual abuser may try to get the kid interested in sex by showing the kid pictures involving sexual activity. The abuser may intentionally talk or act in ways that could cause a kid to have a sexual response.

Some people who try to sexually abuse kids are

adults. Sometimes it might be an older kid or teen who tries to abuse.

Sexual Abuse of Kids by Other Kids (Including Teens)

An older kid should not be attempting to engage in sexual activity with a younger kid. Even if the younger kid consents or initiates it, sexual contact is considered child abuse if there is a *significant age difference* between the two kids.

Sexual relationships between youthful partners need to be limited to *one's own similar-age group*. Questions? Talk to a trusted adult or call Child Help to discuss this:

1-800-4-A-CHILD

For the hearing impaired: 1-800-2-A-CHILD (TTY)

Sexual Abuse of Kids by Adults

It's against the law for an adult to engage in any form of sex play with a kid under any circumstances— even if the kid has a crush and initially tried to attract the adult.

A kid can't make it okay by saying it's okay. The laws against child sexual abuse are made to *protect children*, including children who don't realize that sex with an adult is harmful. It's considered the *adult's fault*—never the kid's fault, no matter what, and the kid doesn't get in trouble when it's reported.

All adults know that it's wrong and illegal to have sex with a kid. An adult who says something different is lying.

Protect Yourself—Say No!

Child abusers are often discouraged from acting when they see that a kid will assert his or her right to say no.

You may have been taught to be respectful of adults. Do *not* be polite or respectful to an adult who tries to have sexual contact with you. Say no! And say it in whatever way you think will be most effective in getting the person to *leave you alone*.

Even if you are frightened or embarrassed, even if you have been threatened or intimidated, even if you are afraid no one will believe you because you have no witnesses to back you up—tell. And keep telling— someone *will* believe you.

Tell right away, without waiting or worrying about the consequences. Tell a parent or other adult relative, your doctor, the police, your teacher, your principal, a nurse, or any other adult you choose. Your only job is to tell, and keep on telling until someone listens.

And don't keep the secret if a friend or sibling tells *you* about abuse.

This is the number of the Child Help IOF Forester's National Child Abuse Hotline:

1-800-4-A-CHILD

For the hearing impaired: **1-800-2-A-CHILD (TTY)**

This hotline is set up to help children and teens with *any kind of abuse, including sexual abuse, physical or emotional abuse, and neglect.*

Anyone with questions or concerns about abuse can call at any time of the day or night. It's free, and the call won't appear on the phone bill.

If you call the hotline, you will get to talk to a trained professional. *Stay on the line.* Keep waiting, and soon a trained professional will answer and help you.

If you, or any child you know, has a problem with being abused, call the hotline number above, the police, or your county's *child protective services.* (Dial "0" or 411, and ask the operator for the number. Or look in the phone book in "county government" listings under "social services," or in the white pages under "child protective services.") Or call a youth crisis hotline (see page 64).

If you need emergency help, call 911 or the police emergency number.

TRUST YOUR OWN INSTINCTS

Kids almost always have an instinctive feeling that something is wrong when an adult (or significantly older kid) tries to start up sexual contact. It's very important to pay attention to those gut feelings. It *seems* wrong because it *is* wrong!

Even a young kid can have enormous power against a person who attempts abuse. The power lies in trusting the feeling that something is wrong, saying no, and reporting what happened. Right away! (see pages 163–164).

Who Could Be a Child Abuser?

Some people think of a child abuser (molester) as a "dirty old man"—but a child abuser can be young or old, clean or dirty, male or female, rich or poor, gay, straight, or bisexual. Most are heterosexual males.

Abusers can be adults, adolescents, or children.

Some child abusers are strangers to the child. But a child abuser can be a person known to the child and/or the child's family. He or she can be a relative— even a parent or older sibling.

A child abuser can be in a position of authority, like a teacher, coach, or religious leader. Often, child abusers get jobs or work as volunteers in situations where they will have easy access to children.

An Example of How a Child Molester Might Act

A person who wants to have sexual contact with a kid may try to befriend the kid (and the kid's family) by doing nice things and maybe offering to take the kid fun places.

After gaining trust, the person then tries to start up a sexual relationship with the kid. The abuser hopes the kid will feel confused, embarrassed, disappointed, humiliated, ashamed, or afraid. The molester gambles that because of these feelings, the kid won't tell. And he or she also gambles on something else: that the kid will somehow feel responsible and will blame himself or herself.

The kid is never responsible, and never to blame.

The Key to Safety Is Communication

Good communication with parents can help avoid situations that might possibly lead to an abuse attempt. If any person or any situation makes you feel uncomfortable, worried, sad, confused, or afraid, tell your parents. If the bad feelings involve a parent, tell your other parent, your doctor, a teacher, or another adult you trust. *Don't wait.*

Incest and Sexual Child Abuse

Sexual relationships between an adult and his or her child, stepchild, nephew, niece, grandchild, or step-grandchild are considered harmful to the child and are against the law in all cases *with no exceptions*, even if the child is willing. It's referred to as *incest,* and it's sexual child abuse.

Sexual relationships between siblings, stepsiblings, and half siblings are also considered incest.

Some children who are victims of incest are afraid to tell because they think that the family will be damaged if they do tell, and they're afraid that the relative who is abusing them may go to jail.

A family is already damaged when a child is suffering from abuse. When abuse is reported, the family can begin the healing process. The abuser is forced to confront his or her problems, often by participating in therapy or other programs prescribed by the court.

In some cases, after an abuser gets treatment and counseling, it is possible for the family to be reunited under the supervision of a court—as long as everyone, including the child, is convinced that the abuse won't happen again.

Sometimes, the child is afraid of the abuser. The

police, the people who work for child protective services, and the counselors who answer the calls on the child abuse hotline can make immediate moves to protect children in all abuse situations.

Trained adults can help a child and his or her family take steps to overcome the pain, fear, and confusion associated with incest and child abuse. They know how hard it is for a child to ask for help in these situations, especially if the abuse involves a relative. Don't keep incest a secret! See the Child Help IOF Forester's National Child Abuse Hotline box on page 164.

Abduction

Abduction is when someone takes someone away by forcing or tricking them. It is *very* unlikely that someone would try to abduct you. But these things are good to know:

Be suspicious of any adult or older teen who asks you for assistance or advice; adults should ask *adults* for help, not *kids*. Don't interact. If a vehicle stops near you and someone calls to you, or motions for you to come closer, move back and be ready to run.

Beware of adults or older teens you don't know well who want to show you interesting things, like cute puppies or motorcycles or lost kitties. Don't be lured away!

If you discover that something of yours, like your bike or pack, has been moved close to a vehicle or close to a place where someone could be hiding, just leave it there. Don't walk up to it. Go to a safe place and call the police or an adult you trust.

There have been cases in which people who abduct children have posed as authority figures. Uniforms are easy to buy or rent. Unless there is a clear public safety emergency involving uniformed police and/or the fire department, or unless *you* need to approach a uniformed officer for help or information, regard someone in a uniform as you would any other stranger. If someone in a uniform approaches you, stay back. *Don't go anywhere* with him or her.

If you see a car circling the block or cruising your street, or if you keep seeing the same car in different places, report it to the police.

If you think someone is following you, keep your distance. Run to a safe place. Get the attention of other adults around you. Remember: Most adults will instinctively protect children and teens in danger— but you need to yell for help when you need help. Use your voice when you sense danger, and use your head. If your safety becomes threatened, do whatever is necessary to get the attention of the community, including setting off car or other alarms.

If grabbed by someone, pull away, fast! Run away from the person, and yell "I don't know you!" or "Somebody, help me!" or "Call 911!" Cause the biggest scene you can so that other people around can hear that you're in trouble and can protect you. Most abductors will run away if the person they are trying to abduct resists and alerts other people.

The National Center for Missing and Exploited Children

There is a national center set up to help all missing, lost, abandoned, abducted, or runaway children. Every family and community wants missing children returned—no matter how far away they may be from home, no matter how long they've been gone, and no matter what has happened to them while they were gone. The National Center for Missing and Exploited Children Hotline number is:

1-800-843-5678 (U.S. and Canada)
1-800-826-7653 (TTY)

❀ Safety Reminders for When You're on Your Own • • • • • • • • •

- Being alert, cautious, and prepared helps keep you safe when you are out in the world. Remember: Acquaintances, not just strangers, can pose a threat to safety.

- Do not accept rides or enter vehicles without your parents' permission.

- Never go anywhere alone, even a short distance, inside or outside, with an adult or older teen you don't know well.

- Say no and tell your parents if someone you don't know well asks you to pose for a picture or be in a film; asks you to give them your name, address, or school name; offers you a job or gift; offers you alcohol or other drugs.

- Don't take shortcuts through alleys, wooded areas, creek beds, railroad tracks, or other out-of-the-way places where you can't be seen and heard. Avoid parking lots and parking garages. Always try to remain in view and earshot of other people who could come to your aid if you needed to call out for help.

- If you become separated from your family, friends, or other group in an unfamiliar area, call 911 (or dial "0" and ask the operator to connect you with the police). Or ask someone who works in a store (wearing a nametag or working as a cashier) to call the police for you. Wait there. The police will come to you as soon as they know where you are. Don't wander in the streets searching—phone the police and wait in a safe place.

- If you go shopping with your friends, choose a *safe* meeting place to go to if you get separated. Go there right away if you do get separated.

- If you're out with your friends and there's a change of plans, call a parent to discuss it. Your parents should know *where you are and whom you're with.*

- Don't allow people you don't know well to engage you in conversation when you are out alone or with your friends. You have no obligation to be polite or interact—so don't.

- Don't "get an attitude," make personal remarks, comment on appearance, or say or do anything else that might provoke a violent response from a kid (or anyone else you don't know). Kids out "looking for a fight" can be dangerous—even armed with weapons. Back off; if you need help from an adult, get help.

- Do not display your name visibly on your clothing or belongings. (It is easier for someone to try to trick you if they know your name.)

Home Alone

- Check to make sure doors and windows are locked.
- Close your blinds or curtains at night. A house or apartment that is lit up inside can be viewed very easily by someone who might be watching from the cover of darkness.

- Don't open the door to anyone you don't know well. If a person hangs around after it is indicated that you won't open the door, call the police emergency number and explain that someone has knocked and isn't leaving.

- To gain entry, people sometimes pretend that there is an emergency and they need to use the phone. If someone knocks on the door and says that there is an emergency, don't open the door. Go straight to the phone and call the police emergency number. The police will tell you what to do.

- Sometimes people pose as repair people to gain entry. A repair should be made when your parent is home, or when proper arrangements have been made in advance with your parent. Don't open the door.

- Know where your parents can be reached. Ask your parents for a trusted neighbor or family friend's number so you can have it handy as a backup while they're gone.

- When you answer the phone, don't give information—get information. If someone asks, "Who's this?" just answer with the question, "Who's calling, please?" If someone asks, "Is your mom or dad home?" say, "Yes, but they're not available to come to the phone. Leave your number, and they'll return the call."

- If you get an obscene phone call (where the caller starts talking about sex or other subjects that are inappropriate or weird), don't speak. Hang up. Report the call to an adult.

Chapter 14

"GIRL THINGS"

REAL PEOPLE

Beautiful people come in all shapes and shades and sizes—and are of all ages; people look like real people, and act like real people! We wake up with our hair sticking out in all directions; our breath isn't always minty fresh; our armpits don't smell like crushed roses.

Be an alert consumer. When you look at ads, remember that you don't have to look like the models you see in ads to be pretty.

And, besides, you don't have to be pretty to be beautiful.

❀ Shopping for Clothes

No matter who you are, there will always be somebody with more expensive, more fashionable, and just plain more clothes than you. It's possible to have a lot of style, even if you don't have much money to spend on fashion.

❧ Hand-me-downs

Wearing hand-me-downs from family or friends is making good use of something that's still wearable. It's a way of recycling and being environmentally conscious.

You might ask your mom or your grandmother if she has something in her jewelry box or closet that she considers out of style, but which is actually now back in style, for kids—like stuff from the sixties and seventies.

Kids are imaginative. It's possible to put together outfits from hand-me-downs or secondhand clothes bought at garage sales, flea markets, and thrift stores. Artists, actors, models, musicians, dancers—even movie stars—have been doing it for years. And if you learn how to sew, you may be able to design or redesign some of your own clothes.

❧ Shopping with a Parent

When you shop with a parent, you might run into some conflicts about what clothes you should wear. This is a normal part of growing up and establishing your identity. I've given up arguing with my daughters. I just go along and sit in a chair, the way my father did when my mother dragged him on shopping expeditions.

A FEW SUGGESTIONS
FOR CLOTHES SHOPPING:

- After buying clothes, keep the tags, the bag, and the receipt until you have tried on everything *at home*. Try it on in front of your mirror. Love it? Still, wait until you've actually made a decision to *wear* it someplace before removing the tags. It's much easier to return clothing when you have the tags, the bag, and the receipt.

- Buy clothing loose enough to fit comfortably after being washed a few times. Washing shrinks stuff, especially cotton. So does the dryer, even on "cool." Regarding pants, shorts, and skirts: Is the waistband tight when you button or snap it? Do the jeans ride up in the rear? If so, don't buy them; you'll be miserable!

- It's not unusual for a girl going through puberty to think her feet are too big. Sometimes feet grow first and the rest of the body catches up later. You may be tempted to buy a smaller shoe size than is actually comfortable, because you want your feet to look smaller. Avoid this temptation! It's bad for your feet to be squeezed into small shoes. There's no advantage in having small feet! Besides, there's only a fraction of an inch difference from one shoe size to the next.

- When you enter a new school year—especially when you start junior high or high school, don't spend all of your "clothes money" before school starts. You may get some fashion ideas from the other kids and wish you'd waited.

- Read labels for washing and cleaning instructions before buying. And keep in mind that dry cleaning costs a fortune!

- Unless you like to iron, think twice about buying clothes that require ironing. If you take your clothes out of the dryer and fold them or hang them on hangers when they're still warm, you can avoid wrinkles.

- If you shop in secondhand stores, give the armpits a "sniff test." If the underarm area doesn't smell good, don't buy it unless you're sure it's washable in hot water and detergent.

High-heeled Shoes

When I was a kid, I admired my mother's high-heeled shoes—in particular, a see-through plastic pair. I liked seeing my mother's feet through the plastic tops, especially her toenails, painted candy-apple red.

One afternoon, without asking permission, I took these lovely shoes for a hike around the second-floor hallway and fell down the stairs. I wasn't hurt. But the shoes were—one heel broke off. Later, I remember seeing the shoes in the trash, with potato peelings on top of them—ruined.

HIGH-
HEELED

MEDIUM
HEEL

LOW-HEEL

There are few things on earth more impractical to wear than high-heeled shoes. They're difficult to walk in, they're often uncomfortable, and they limit normal physical activity to teetering around, standing, and sitting.

If you want heels, start out with a low pair. If you want to look and feel relaxed, you're going to have to log some walking time—and learn to climb stairs. Walk around the house before attempting to walk through a sixth-grade graduation ceremony or other important social event. In time, you'll get the hang of it. When you practice on the stairs, hold on to the rail on the way up and on the way down. *Always put your hand on the rail before starting down a flight of stairs.*

One time-worn solution to high-heeled shoes is to buy them for that special occasion—and then temporarily ditch them someplace, such as in a potted plant. A better solution: Wear dressy flat shoes. Boys don't totter around in heels. Why should girls?

PANTY*hose*

Struggling into a pair of pantyhose isn't everybody's favorite thing to do. But many of us have occasion to wear them.

Before you buy pantyhose, study the size chart or guide on the back of the package. It has been my experience that pantyhose are fairly skimpy; sometimes it's best to go one size bigger than the package suggests.

Before you put on pantyhose, check your fingernails and toenails to make sure you don't have any rough edges. Pantyhose snag easily, and the snag will cause a "run," which is a runaway line that zooms upward through the sheer fabric. When a run is first starting, you may be able to save the day by dabbing a little clear nail polish at the tip of the run.

Put on pantyhose one leg at a time. First, hold them up to make sure the tag is in the back of the waistband (or the feet are facing in the right direction). Gather your way down the leg—bunching it up until you're holding the whole leg by the foot—then put your foot in carefully. Slowly pull the pantyhose up that leg until you get about halfway up the thigh. Do the same with the other leg. Then move 'em on up to your waist.

If you need more room at the top of the pantyhose, gather it down by the ankle, and slowly bring it up to the top. It doesn't do any good to pull from the top—in fact, that's a good way to rip or run them.

✿

GARTER BELTS

Pantyhose took over for garter belts and nylon stockings about thirty years ago, although recently it seems that garter belts are trying to make a comeback.

A garter belt goes around the waist and (usually) hooks in the back. Garters hang down on elastic ribbons; these attach to stockings, to hold them up.

✿ Shaving

There is no need for people to shave their legs or underarms, and many women don't.

If you want to shave the hair off your legs, underarms, or both, get permission first. Ask for a demonstration, if you haven't already had the chance to watch. Don't shave facial hair. It grows right back and will feel stubbly. There are products available to bleach facial hair. Ask permission before using them and follow the directions carefully. Never allow bleach to get near or in your eyes.

❀ Electric Razors

Don't use electric razors or any other appliances near water—you could get electrocuted (shocked to death).

Certain *battery-operated* electric razors are designed to get wet. They say "wet/dry" or "fully submersible" on them. If an electric razor doesn't have those words on it, *don't get it wet.*

❀ Disposable (Throwaway) Razors

Disposable razors are popular and relatively safe to use—although it's easy with any razor to nick or cut yourself while shaving. Disposable razors should not be used more than a few times—and should not be shared.

- A good place to shave with a disposable razor is in the bathtub. You will need to get your legs wet and soapy. Some women use shaving cream or gel.

- Lather up one leg, then slowly and carefully shave a little at a time, starting from your ankle. It doesn't require much pressure to shave, so don't push down too hard. Stop every once in a while to rinse the hair off the razor.

- To shave your underarms, wet and soap them, then carefully shave off the hair. Don't move the razor sideways; it's easier to nick your skin that way. Wait a while to apply deodorant after shaving your underarms. You'll feel a stinging sensation otherwise.

✿ DEPILATORIES

Depilatories are lotions or creams that chemically dissolve body hair near the root. They are easy to use: rub the cream or lotion into the skin, leave on for a short period of time, then rinse off. Some depilatories, however, have a strong smell. And some people are allergic to the ingredients in depilatories, so be sure to do a patch test on a small area of skin first. Follow directions carefully—and ask permission before using depilatories.

Waxing

Waxing is another way to remove unwanted hair, including facial hair, without shaving. It's also used to "adjust" the bikini line, which refers to the pubic hair that peeks out of a bathing suit.

Warm, waxy goop is applied, then pulled off after it hardens, yanking out the hairs. Ouch! Not only does waxing hurt, but occasionally infections and skin irritation can result. Should you decide to have waxing done in a salon, have your parent accompany you.

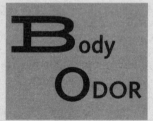

Growing up includes smelling stronger than you did when you were a little kid. Changes in hormones cause you to sweat, or perspire, more freely. If you bathe regularly, you'll smell great.

Beware of perfumed products, including those lovely little soaps, bubble bath powders, bath beads, and other good-smelling products developed for use in the bathtub. Many girls and women find that their skin is too tender for these products. They can be especially irritating to your vaginal area. If you try them, use just a little at a time and rinse well.

You may have reached the point at which your armpits get damp and smell musty when you sweat. The smell of sweat is natural, but many people choose to cover it up with a deodorant/antiperspirant.

ROLL-ON

SPRAY

CREAM IN A POT

STICK

Deodorants/antiperspirants are available in various forms—spray, cream, stick, and roll-on. They all work pretty much the same. Some are scented, some aren't.

If, for some reason, you don't have the opportunity to jump in the shower or bath as often as you'd like, or if you want or need to conserve water, you can give yourself a sponge bath with warm water, soap, and a washcloth.

Do it as my mom did: armpits—wash then rinse; crotch—wash then rinse; and rear—wash then rinse. Don't reverse the order; wash and rinse your rear last. And while we're on the subject: When you go to the bathroom, wipe from front to rear. This prevents germs from the anus from sneaking over into your vagina, where they can multiply and cause infections.

✿ SKIN PRODUCTS

Lotion and sunblock are two products for skin that you might want to keep on hand.

Whatever the shade of your skin, it's the right shade. If you see an ad that suggests you should change your skin color, don't fall for it. Nobody's skin is too dark or too light. A little lotion will make dry skin feel soft and smooth and will bring out the rich tones of the skin.

The lighter your skin and the lighter your eyes, the better your chance of developing skin cancer from exposure to the ultraviolet rays of the sun. Having dark skin and eyes may make you less susceptible to skin cancer, but by no means immune. Exposure to the sun can also cause damaging sunburns and premature aging of the skin.

It's unhealthy to darken the skin by basking in the sun. Wear sunblock when you're going to be out in the sun. Wear waterproof sunblock when you're swimming. And beware of tanning salons. Tans fade, but the unhealthy effects of exposure to ultraviolet rays linger on.

IF YOU'RE INTERESTED IN MAKEUP

- *Lipstick* is used to make lips shine or not shine, and/or to make the lips a different color. *Lipliner*, usually found in pencil form, more strongly defines the shape of the lips and is often used along with lipstick of a similar shade.

- *Foundation* can be liquid or a creamy solid. It is worn to cover up little bumps and marks on the skin and to make skin look smooth. Foundation is available to match and complement all skin shades and tones, from the darkest to the lightest. Oil-free, water-based foundation is available.

- *Powder* can be pressed or loose, and the purpose of wearing it is to make skin look unshiny. It can be worn over foundation or used by itself.

- *Blush* is usually worn near the cheekbones. It adds color.

- *Eyeliner* can be liquid, in which case it is drawn on with the little brush that comes with it, or it can be solid, in the shape of a pencil. Eyeliner can be drawn along the eyelid just above the upper eyelashes and just below the lower lashes. Its purpose is to emphasize the eyes.

- *Mascara* is brushed on with a little applicator brush and makes eyelashes look darker and, sometimes, thicker and longer. If you use mascara, apply it slowly and carefully. Poking yourself in the eye with the mascara brush hurts and can harm your eye.
- *Eyebrow pencil* is used to define the shape of the eyebrows and make them look darker.
- *Eye shadow* is usually brushed onto the eyelid and below the eyebrow; sometimes colors are blended.

Infections such as pinkeye (conjunctivitis) can be spread by sharing eye makeup. Lipstick can also carry germs that can be passed from one person to another. If you don't want to share your makeup—don't.

Some makeup is hypoallergenic, which means it is less likely to irritate the skin. Regardless of what kind of makeup you use, if you notice a skin irritation, stop using the product. If the irritation persists, talk to a doctor.

Hair Products

You may enjoy experimenting with curlers, curling irons, crimpers, pigtails, ponytails, braids, cornrows, extensions, weaves, waves, French twists, conditioning caps, oils, styling gels and foams, ribbons, barrettes, or bows.

Hair grows naturally in a variety of colors and textures. In almost every fashion magazine, you will see a hairstyle that takes a minimum of effort to maintain; these hairstyles are based on the idea that all hair can look great in its natural state.

You can get ideas for hairstyles by looking through magazines and books in the library. Some magazines have special sections on hair care and styling.

Some styles require the expertise of a professional stylist; others can be done at home with the help of an adult; and some you can do yourself.

There are many products sold that alter the natural state of hair. Ask permission before using these. *Read the warning label on the package carefully before you buy*. Most, such as perms, relaxers, bleaches, and dyes, require adult supervision. Study the warnings on the packaging and follow all directions, especially regarding your eyes. Don't dye or bleach eyelashes or eyebrows!

If you accidentally get a potentially damaging hair product in your eyes, *immediately* begin flushing your eyes with water. Catch a *gentle* stream from the faucet in your hand and blink into it, use an eye cup, or ask a helper to pour water *gently* into your eye from a clean cup. Continue *flushing your eyes for fifteen minutes*—then call the doctor or poison control number for additional advice. The poison control number for your region will probably be listed on the emergency page in the front of the phone book. Or, call the information operator for the number.

✿ Poor Richard

Within just a few weeks, my friend Richard—father of five kids—accidentally brushed his teeth with a big gob of Desitin (diaper rash medicine that comes in a tube), accidentally slathered his armpits with his wife's roll-on spot remover (he thought it was deodorant), and accidentally lathered himself up in the shower with flea soap (he thought it was somebody's "zit soap").

Thankfully, most adults have better bathroom survival skills than Richard—but little kids don't.

If you have younger siblings or visit friends with

younger siblings, keep your purse and makeup kit out of reach. Don't leave your special stuff out on the bathroom counter. Little kids are nosy; they get into stuff—especially when it smells delicious. Many delicious-smelling cosmetics are poisonous.

> Now that you're growing up and have more grown-up things, you'll need to keep nail polish remover, nail polish, skin care products, hair care products, makeup, fancy soap and other bath products, and—of course—all medication out of the reach of children.

Farewell

Years have passed since my first Ladies' Business Club meetings with my mom. I'm forty-eight now. I wear a little mascara and eyeshadow. I wear a little dark lipstick, when I can find it.

I don't wear dresses.

Most of the time, I wear jeans, Ben Davis shirts, a wedding ring, and Doc Marten boots.

After supper, I sit on the porch and wait for the owls to hoot.

My breasts never grew huge.

When I climb into the bathtub, I displace more water than I used to. If I had time, I would still enjoy soaping up my belly and drawing on it.

My daughters storm into the bathroom when I'm in there. Of course, when they're in the bathroom, they always lock me out: club rules.

I called my mom a few days ago and asked her if

it really, *really* was okay if I wrote about how she looked, naked, in a book.

"Are you going to say how you look, naked, in a book?" she asked me.

"I don't know," I told her.

"Well, if you'll go naked, I'll go naked."

"Okay," I told her. "But you're changing the club rules!"

Naked, I look a lot like how my mom looked when I was ten: like a naked, middle-aged mom.

And, one day, I'll look like how my mom looks now: with two beautiful, round twinkly eyes and, best of all, cheeks warmer and softer than toasted marshmallows.

By the time I look like how my mom looks now, you might have daughters of your own—or sons, who hide athletic supporters under notebooks and sweaters.

But for now you're still a kid.

You might look a little like how I looked when I was a kid: two small-, medium-, or large-sized breasts with brown-, pink-, or plum-colored nipples, a carpet or cloud of pubic hair: straight or curly, black, brown, red, or blond.

You're a kid: breasts, new body hair, and having a period doesn't change that. Looking like an adult doesn't mean that you're expected to take on adult roles and responsibilities. You're a kid, entitled to the love, care, and protection of the adults around you.

Take good care of your spirit; communicate with your friends, family, teachers, and health care professionals—especially about things that may trouble you or confuse you, or that make you feel afraid or sad.

Take good care of your body; it contains something miraculous—you. Don't do drugs. Eat well. Wear your seat belt. Wear your bicycle helmet and other protective gear for sports. Don't let anyone who's been using drugs or alcohol drive you anywhere.

Postpone having sex with a partner.

You're growing up—and there's lots to learn. And you've got lots of time to learn it. Stay informed, so you can stay in charge. Ask questions. Read books and magazines. Stay in school. Gather information, so you can make decisions that will help to keep you safe and strong.

Think for yourself! Don't give in to the feeling that you "have to" do what other kids are doing in order to "belong." You belong!

Accept yourself. Hear your own ideas and pay attention to your own instincts about what is right, or wrong, for you.

WORK HARD

WORK

PLAY HARD

HARD

Play HARD

MAKE PLANS

MAKE

DREAM.

PLANS

DrEAM

Dream.

For Further Reading

Guidebooks

Adolescence and Growing Up

Bell, Alison, and Lisa Rooney, M.D. *Your Body, Yourself: A Guide to Your Changing Body* (Los Angeles: Lowell House, 1993).

Bell, Ruth. *Changing Bodies, Changing Lives* (New York: Vintage Books, 1988).

Fenwick, Elizabeth, and Richard Walker. *How Sex Works: A Clear, Comprehensive Guide for Teenagers to Emotional, Physical, and Sexual Maturity* (New York: Dorling Kindersley, 1994).

Gardner-Loulan, JoAnn, and Bonnie Lopez. *Period* (Volcano, Calif.: Volcano Press, 1991). Includes a removable parents' guide.

Harris, Robie H. *It's Perfectly Normal: Changing Bodies, Growing Up, Sex, & Sexual Health* (Cambridge, Mass.: Candlewick Press, 1994).

Lauerson, Niels H., M.D., Ph.D., and Eileen Stukane. *You're in Charge: A Teenage Girl's Guide to Sex and Her Body* (New York: Fawcett Columbine, 1993).

Madaras, Lynda. *My Feelings, My Self: Lynda Madaras's Growing-Up Guide for Girls* (New York: Newmarket Press, 1993).

Madaras, Lynda. *The What's Happening to My Body? Book for Girls: A Growing-Up Guide for Parents and Daughters* (New York: Newmarket Press, 1988).

Marzollo, Jean. *Getting Your Period: A Book About Menstruation* (New York: Dial Books for Young Readers, 1989).

McCoy, Kathy, and Charles Wibbelsman. *The New Teenage Body Book* (New York: Perigee Books, 1992).

Powledge, Fred. *You'll Survive: Late Blooming, Early Blooming, Loneliness, Klutziness, and Other Problems of Adolescence, and How to Live Through Them* (New York: Scribner's, 1986).

Information About Drugs, Alcohol, and Cigarettes

Hyde, Margaret O. *Know About Drugs* (New York: Walker & Company, 1990).

Hyde, Margaret O. *Know About Smoking* (New York: Walker & Company, 1990).

Langone, John. *Tough Choices: A Book About Substance Abuse* (Boston: Little, Brown and Company, 1995).

Information About HIV/AIDS

Blake, Jeanne. *Risky Times: How to Be AIDS-Smart and Stay Healthy: A Guide for Teenagers* (New York: Workman Publishing, 1990).

Ford, Michael Thomas. *100 Questions and Answers About AIDS: What You Need to Know Now* (New York: Macmillan Publishing, 1993).

Ford, Michael Thomas. *The Voices of AIDS: Twelve Unforgettable People Talk About How AIDS Has Changed Their Lives* (New York: William Morrow & Company, 1995).

Hyde, Margaret O., and Elizabeth H. Forsyth, M.D. *AIDS: What Does It Mean to You?* (New York: Walker & Company, 1992).

Johnson, Earvin "Magic." *What You Can Do to Avoid AIDS* (New York: Times Books, 1992).

Madaras, Lynda. *Lynda Madaras Talks to Teens About AIDS: An Essential Guide for Parents, Teachers, and Young People* (New York: Newmarket Press, 1988).

Recovering from Crisis, Including Death and Rape

Bode, Janet. *Death Is Hard to Live With* (New York: Bantam Books, 1993).

Bode, Janet. *The Voices of Rape* (New York: Franklin Watts, 1990).

Zvirin, Stephanie. *The Best Years of Their Lives: A Resource Guide for Teenagers in Crisis* (Chicago: American Library Association, 1992).

Self-Esteem/Identity

Blume, Judy. *Letters to Judy: What Your Kids Wish They Could Tell You* (New York: Pocket Books, 1986).

Carlip, Hillary. *Girl Power: Young Women Speak Out! Writings from Teenage Girls* (New York: Warner Books, 1995).

Corbette, K., and V. Lewis Cupolo. *No More Stares: A Role Model Book for Disabled Teenage Girls* (Berkeley, Calif.: Disability Rights Education Defense Fund, 1982).

Duvall, Lynn. *Respecting Our Differences: A Guide to Getting Along in a Changing World* (Minneapolis: Free Spirit Publishing, 1994).

Karnes, Frances A., and Suzanne M. Bean. *Girls and Young Women Leading the Way: Twenty True Stories About Leadership* (Minneapolis: Free Spirit Publishing, 1993).

Palmer, Dr. Pat. *Teen Esteem: A Self-Direction Manual for Young Adults* (San Luis Obispo, Calif.: Impact Publishers, 1989).

Collections of Stories and Essays

Growing Up Gay and Lesbian

Bauer, Marion Dane, ed. *Am I Blue? Coming Out from the Silence* (New York: HarperCollins, 1994).

Due, Linnea. *Joining the Tribe: Growing Up Gay & Lesbian in the '90s* (New York: Anchor Books, 1995).

Sutton, Roger. *Hearing Us Out: Voices from the Gay and Lesbian Community* (Boston: Little, Brown and Company, 1994).

Collections About Growing Up and Cultural Identity

Bolden, Tonya, ed. *Rites of Passage: Stories About Growing Up by Black Writers from Around the World* (New York: Hyperion Books for Children, 1994).

Carlson, Lori M., ed. *American Eyes: New Asian-American Short Stories for Young Adults* (New York: Henry Holt & Company, 1994).

Carlson, Lori M., ed. *Cool Salsa: Bilingual Poems on Growing Up Latino in the United States* (New York: Henry Holt & Company, 1995).

Pamphlets

The following guides for parents and daughters are available from the Planned Parenthood Federation of America:

Feeling Good About Growing Up (Item 1593)

Having Your Period (Item 1627)

How to Talk to Your Child About Sexuality: A Parent's Guide (Item 1692)

How to Talk with Your Teen About the Facts of Life (Item 1436)

Human Sexuality: What Children Should Know and When They Should Know It (Item 1700)

Teen Sex? It's OK to Say: No Way! (Item 1592)

What If I'm Pregnant? (Item 1925)

Index

About the Author

Mavis Jukes is the award-winning author of several books for children and teenagers, including the Newbery Honor Book *Like Jake and Me, No One Is Going to Nashville, Blackberries in the Dark, Getting Even, Wild Iris Bloom,* and *I'll See You in My Dreams.* She taught school for several years—and became a lawyer—before becoming a children's book writer. Mavis Jukes volunteers as an attorney in the area of juvenile defense and is presently a language arts specialist in a public elementary school. She lives with her husband, the artist Robert Hudson, and their teenage daughters in Sonoma County, California.